Keith Moray is a part-time doctor, columnist and novelist. He lives and works in Wakefield.

FLOTSAM & JETSAM

The Flotsam & Jetsam TV show gained a cult following throughout Scotland by highlighting that money could be made from the debris that washed up onto remote beaches. When it came to West Uist, it brought the exciting prospect of celebrity status for the locals. Then, one fateful night, everything changed . . . The death of a noted scientist, the discovery of a half-drowned puppy and the suggestion of police negligence now lead Inspector Torquil McKinnon to investigate sinister events on the seemingly idyllic island. Who knows what other secrets will be washed ashore?

KEITH MORAY

---◆---

FLOTSAM
& JETSAM

Complete and Unabridged

ULVERSCROFT
Leicester

First published in Great Britain in 2010 by
Robert Hale Limited
London

First Large Print Edition
published 2011
by arrangement with
Robert Hale Limited
London

British Library CIP Data

Moray, Keith.
  Flotsam & jetsam.
  1. Television programs- -Scotland- -Hebrides- -Fiction.
  2. Beachcombing- -Scotland- -Western Isles- -Fiction.
  3. Scientists- -Death- -Fiction. 4. Detective and mystery
  stories. 5. Large type books.
  I. Title
  823.9'2–dc22

  ISBN 978–1–4448–0861–2

Published by
F. A. Thorpe (Publishing)
Anstey, Leicestershire

Set by Words & Graphics Ltd.
Anstey, Leicestershire
Printed and bound in Great Britain by
T. J. International Ltd., Padstow, Cornwall

This book is printed on acid-free paper

For Lily

Prologue

A year ago

He had risen at three, well before the dawn came creeping. Time enough to prepare his porridge and drink his first dram of the day. The fact that he took it with hot water and a teaspoonful of Cascara Sagrada in the guise of a medicinal tonic for his bowels was his way of soothing his conscience and denying the fact that he had a drink problem.

With his tonic by his side he set about preparing his telescope to scan the horizon. The tide would have turned half an hour ago, making it a perfect time to see what fruits and treasures the sea had brought in.

'I will take the *Sea Beastie* out later and check out the Cruadalach Isles. I am feeling in my bones that it will be a good day for beachcombing.' He scratched his grizzled beard and glanced with a grin at the calendar on the nearby desk. 'It should be today, at any rate.'

He sipped his drink then straddled the high stool in eager anticipation.

The darkness began to recede as the rising

1

sun broke the horizon.

As usual the heaps of assorted seaweeds became visible. Then the rocks began peeping above the surf as the departing waters went out quickly. It was then that he saw it at the water's edge, half in and half out of the water. It was long and light coloured. At first he thought it was just another piece of flotsam or jetsam. Timber from a crate or some sort of packaging. Then by the shape he thought it could be a dead seal.

'Bloody hell! Why can't they go and die on someone else's beach!' he grumbled, swinging his telescope round and peering through the eyepiece.

'Jesus!' he exclaimed, adjusting the focus. 'That's no dead seal, but it looks dead enough.'

Through the telescope he saw the naked body of a young woman lying face down, her long blonde hair ebbing too and fro in the puddle around her, the receding waters still playing over her buttocks and legs.

He straightened up and frowned as he pulled a ready-made roll-up from behind his ear and casually lit it with his old Zippo.

'I suppose I had better make sure she is dead,' he grunted to himself. 'Bloody inconvenient, that's what it is.'

He poured another dram, but omitted the

Cascara Sagrada this time. He reconciled it with his conscience that this was not a normal occurrence so he would permit himself some leeway. He smoked and drank for a few minutes then stubbed the cigarette out and drained the glass.

'Sorry, lassie,' he said, rising and stretching his aching muscles. 'One thing is sure: I can't have you cluttering up my beach. You'll have to go.'

He wheezed as he laughed. Then he felt a spasm of pain in his chest. It shot up into his neck and down the left arm.

'And this bloody angina is inconvenient too!' He groaned. 'Oh not now! Not now!'

The pain tightened and he reached for his phone. 'Must — get — help!' he said through gritted teeth. He glanced back out of the window at the body and the effect of the receding surf. It was just as if a frilly white dress was being peeled off her to leave her naked body on the beach.

'Damned — fool — of — a woman!' he gasped. 'Gah!'

1

I

Inspector Torquil McKinnon, 'Piper' to most people on West Uist, had been practising his pipes in St Ninian's Cave. It was something he tried to do at least once a week. On those days, although not normally an early-riser, he would get up with the first light, have a frugal breakfast then ride down to the cave before he went in to the police station in Kyleshiffin. He found it an excellent way of problem-solving.

For ten minutes he ran through his repertoire of warm-up exercises, to get his finger movements right. He played a string of ever more complex movements — leumluaths, taorluaths, gracenotes and birls. Then he played a strathspey and reel, then a hornpipe before concentrating on the piobaireachd, the pibroch.

The great basalt columned St Ninian's Cave had been used by generations of island pipers, including Torquil's uncle, the Reverend Lachlan McKinnon. They had lived together in the old manse ever since Torquil's parents had died in a boating accident when he was a youngster and Lachlan had been appointed as his guardian. He remembered the day when Lachlan had taken him and his pipes and introduced him to the cave's special magic. The young Torquil had hoped that he would one day follow in his uncle's footsteps and become a champion piper and winner of the Silver Quaich. Much to their mutual pleasure he duly did, just a year before, so that there now resided a Silver Quaich on each end of the mantelpiece in the manse's sitting-room.

Nature had carved this sea cave beautifully, so that it seemed to hold a sound perfectly for a moment so that the piper was able to hear the correct pitch of his playing. It was a natural tape recorder for a musician.

Suddenly a sour note from a faulty fingering grated around the cave.

'Och! It is all rubbish that you are playing, Torquil McKinnon. You are playing like a constipated crow today,' he chided himself as he let the blow pipe drop from his lips then gave the bag a sharp chop so that it was instantly silenced as the reeds closed, rather than producing the amateurish moaning as the bag slowly deflated that bagpipe loathers likened to the death throes of a dying sheep. He shook his head and bit his lower lip.

'Too much on my mind, that is the trouble.'

He was a tall twenty-nine year old man with coal-black hair, high cheekbones and a slightly hawk-like nose. He had been the youngest inspector in the whole of the Western Isles and to many a West Uist lass he had been considered a desirable and eligible male. That had changed relatively recently when he lost his heart to Sergeant Lorna Golspie. Things had been so good between them over the last few weeks until his superior officer had thrown a spanner in the works.

Torquil felt his temper begin to rise, but he suppressed it quickly. He stood for a moment and reverently bent his head, much as he would in his uncle's church.

'*Tapadh leat*! Thank you!' he said to the great columned chamber, itself like a church. The Padre himself had taught him to show respect to St Ninian and his cave for in a way it was the best teacher a piper could ever have.

With his pipes under his arm he left the cave and crunched up the kelp-covered shingle beach towards the lay-by above where he had parked his classic Royal Enfield Bullet 500.

'Damn Superintendent Lumsden!' he said

7

to himself. 'Why could you not just let us have some time together instead of seconding her to the Lewis station. As if they didn't have enough — '

He stopped short when he heard the moan. It sounded like a dog whimpering.

He spun round and looked in the direction of the sea. The tide had turned some time ago and was going out, exposing heaps of seaweed-covered rocks and leaving countless pools.

Floating in one such pool was a piece of timber. To his horror he saw that a young three-coloured collie, little more than a puppy was lying sprawled on the timber, lashed to it with several loops of thick cord. Its fur was soaked and spiky and it looked exhausted. Its weary eyes were fixed on him and it raised its head and whimpered pitifully.

'*Creideamh*! Faith!' Torquil exclaimed, laying his bagpipes down on the shingle and sprinting over towards the pool where the timber-bound dog was bobbing up and down. 'Who would do such a thing. They meant to drown you?'

Without hesitation he jumped into the pool despite his heavy-buckled Ashman boots and waded over to retrieve the timber and the animal. He hoisted the timber and the dog out of the water and waded back. Once he had climbed out, he examined the cord, observing as he did that it had been looped around the dog's body several times and tied with knots that he was unfamiliar with. They certainly did not seem to be common seamen's knots, yet they had been competently formed and were intended not to slip.

'It looks like someone knew what they were doing, my wee friend,' he said. He pulled out a penknife and sliced the ropes distant from the knots. He had half expected the dog to make a bolt for freedom, but it just lay on the timber and continued to moan. Then it started to shiver.

'You are too exhausted to move, I think. And you must have been in the water a long time judging by the state of you. I am surprised that you have survived the cold.' And after reassuringly stroking its coat and trying to get some of the excess water from its fur, he pulled off the navy-blue Arran jumper that was the only concession to a uniform that he made and wrapped the dog in it. Stuffing the ropes into his pocket he carried it and the timber back up the beach. Then he tossed the timber above the high water-line and picked up his pipes.

'A good thing I have two panniers on the Bullet,' he told the shivering creature a few moments later as he stowed first the dog into one, then his pipes into the other carrier. He pulled on his gauntlets, wrapped his McKinnon tartan scarf about his neck and pulled on his Cromwell helmet. He grinned at the steadily rising sun.

'And a good thing that you are there to warm us up, master sun, otherwise I would not relish riding to Kylshiffin in my T-shirt.' Then, nodding at the dog, 'We'll have a better look at you back at the station, my wee friend. I would like to know who your owner is and why he or she tried to murder you.'

He kicked the Bullet into action and moments later he opened up the throttle and was accelerating along the snaking headland road past Loch Hynish on his way to Kyleshiffin.

He had been cross about Superintendent Lumsden, but attempted murder in any form, even of a dog, made his blood boil.

II

Ordinarily the Padre, as Torquil's uncle, the Reverend Lachlan McKinnon, was known by most folk, was careful about the times he played golf in the summer. While the early hours after dawn were a good time to play in the autumn and the spring, he tended to tee-off later in the day during the summer months. But when one had a guest priest in the parish it was another matter. One had to be hospitable and play nine holes when they wanted to. When the guest played off a suspiciously high handicap and was well known for liking a bet on a game there was even more reason to be accommodating. Lachlan was a canny player himself and he hoped that his local knowledge of the course would come in useful.

So far the match was all square. They had teed off at 6 and played seven holes before 7.15.

'Sure, it is a real golfing paradise that you have here on West Uist, Lachlan,' said the Reverend Kenneth Canfield, the chaplain to the University of the Highlands as he lined up a six foot putt then gently stroked the ball into the hole. 'Par four,' he said with glee, nimbly bending and collecting his ball.

He was a slim, wiry man in his late forties, a former Scottish Universities squash champion. He had a good eye for a ball, but had only been playing golf for about five years. Lachlan thought that his middle handicap belied his ability and suspected that he 'protected it' at his home club. The collection of trophies that he had seen in his study when he had last visited him in Inverness seemed to support that.

11

'Aye, it may not be St Andrews, but it is a fair test of golf, Kenneth.' He lined up his own putt and similarly tapped the ball in. 'And a par for me too. Still all square. Now for the long eighth. I warn you, it is a wee tester.'

Lachlan was proud of the ten-acre plot of undulating dunes and machair that he and several other local worthies had years before transformed into the St Ninian's Golf Course. Using the natural lie of the land they had constructed six holes, each with at least two potential hazards. The fairways were tractor-mown once a week, the greens were sheep-grazed to near billiard table smoothness and the bunkers (in the beginning at least) had been excavated by generations of rabbits. Each hole had three separate tee positions, each one giving its route to the hole a special name in both English and Gaelic, thereby allowing players the choice of playing a conventional eighteen holes or any combination they chose.

The Padre had tended his flock for more years than he cared to think about. He was now sixty-four years of age and especially proud of the fact that he played off a golf handicap exactly one eighth of his age, having been a single figure handicapper all of his adult life.

He was a tall man, with a mop of shaggy white hair that seemed to defy the application of brush or comb, who sported a pair of horn-rimmed spectacles. He was dressed in his usual attire which he wore both on and off the golf course; a green West Uist tweed jacket, corduroy trousers, black shirt and a dog-collar.

They crossed from the green to the eighth tee. A stone marker had a plaque, proclaiming that the hole was called Carragh, the Pillar, because of an ancient standing stone that rose out of the rough on the left of the fairway.

'You will see that the hole plays entirely differently from this tee, Kenneth,' Lachlan volunteered as he shoved a tee peg in the ground and pulled out his trusty two wood. 'You will need to keep to the fairway if you want to make sure that you avoid the Pillar.'

He addressed the ball then swung freely and effortlessly. There was a satisfying click of wood on ball then he held his follow-through and watched the ball start out right then slowly draw back towards the middle of the fairway. It bounced then ran on for another forty yards, rolling just beyond the Pillar.

'I don't know how you manage to hit the ball so far and so accurately with those old wooden-headed clubs of yours,' Kenneth

13

said, with an admiring shake of the head. 'Good drive!'

'Thank you, Kenneth,' Lachlan replied. 'The truth is that I have never fancied those newfangled metal woods. It sounds like you are hitting the ball with a tin can.'

The Reverend Canfield teed up his ball. 'But at least they are quite forgiving. They have a bigger sweet spot and I think they make a difference in length.' He pulled out his huge-headed driver. 'In fact, I am going to ignore your advice and try the tiger line. If I can cut off a bit of the dog-leg I could maybe get my trusty eight iron to the green with my second shot. Then with the stroke you are giving me on the hole . . . '

He winked meaningfully then addressed his ball. He swung fast and hard, fairly relishing the noise that Lachlan so scorned. The ball shot off in the direction of the Pillar, easily clearing it to land in the short rough near a thicket of yellow blossomed gorse bushes on the left of the fairway, a good thirty yards further on than Lachlan's ball.

'Excellent shot,' Lachlan enthused. 'Fortune favours the brave. You should have an easy shot to the green with your second. Just watch your footing because it tends to be pretty damp over there.'

He pulled out a battered old briar pipe

14

from his breast pocket and started stuffing its bowl with tobacco from a dilapidated yellow oilskin pouch. He struck a light and grinned with amusement as he watched the Reverend Canfield striding after his ball.

You are going to need a bit of good fortune, he mischievously thought to himself. We'll see if you are as fast as you used to be on the squash court.

He ambled on in the direction of his own ball, keeping an eye on his playing partner. He saw him tramp into the rough to find his ball. Then he selected a club from his bag and stood behind the ball with his club held dangling at arm's length, like a plum-bob to get the line to the green.

And, just as the Padre had suspected, it happened. A dark hazy cloud rose from the rough, moving outwards from the gorse bushes towards the Reverend Canfield. Within seconds it engulfed him.

'Gah! Midges!' he cried, frantically scratching his exposed skin. Then he let forth a stream of invective quite unbecoming to one of his cloth.

Despite himself, Lachlan chuckled. Fearful that Kenneth Canfield should hear him he puffed harder on his pipe and soon had billows of smoke around him. 'Are you being attacked, Kenneth?' he called rhetorically.

Kenneth was swiping at the swarm of midges to no avail. In despair he lashed out at the ball with his club and foozled it a few yards ahead. With a scowl he shouldered his bag, ran on to the ball and swiped again, with similar result. Eventually, after three more such attempts, he made it to the fairway, finally leaving the midge swarm behind him.

Lachlan knocked an easy five iron into the heart of the green.

'I wish I had known that you had a midge problem over on that side of the course,' Kenneth said plaintively.

Lachlan noticed the suspicious glint in his eye, but feigned surprise. 'Oh well, Kenneth, you are in the Outer Hebrides. The whole of the west of Scotland has a midge problem as you know. All you can do is try to avoid them.'

'Or keep them away with a foul-smelling pipe!'

Lachlan laughed. 'With all these new anti-smoking laws the golf course is about the only place left where you are allowed to smoke. The fact that the *meanbh-chuileag*, the 'tiny fly' doesn't like my tobacco is quite fortuitous.' He watched as Kenneth selected a seven iron and addressed his ball.

'Maybe you should have checked on Dr Digby Dent's Midge Index before coming out this morning?' Lachlan suggested.

To his surprise Kenneth glared at him, and then took a wild swipe at his ball. The result was inevitable. He hit a duck hook that sent the ball arcing viciously in the direction of the rough and more gorse bushes on the left. It disappeared into them.

'Pah! It is no good. I concede this hole Lachlan. Why did you have to mention that man's name?'

'Dr Dent?' Lachlan returned with mild surprise. 'Have you a problem with him, Kenneth? Why he seems a decent enough chap to me. He must be the world's foremost expert on the midge. In fact, I am planning to go to hear him talk tonight. He is doing a short spot on that Scottish TV show that they are shooting on the island over the next two weeks. *Flotsam & Jetsam* it is called. I was going to suggest that you come along?'

'Ah yes, that antique and junk show with the tanned chappie with the world's worst wig and the glamorous partner. I have seen an episode or two when they came to Inverness. So what is my university's famous entomologist doing on this show?'

Lachlan tapped his pipe out on the blade of his putter and grinned. 'Explaining about midges, would you believe?'

The Reverend Kenneth Canfield smiled

back. 'In that case I wouldn't miss him for the world.'

But Lachlan noted the tinge of sarcasm in his voice that belied the smile.

III

Fergus Ferguson was used to being recognized. Camera-shy he definitely was not. In fact, he felt totally at home in front of a lens, which undoubtedly had something to do with his great success as a TV presenter. Although he thought it a bit of a mouthful, he revelled in being known as the doyen of the antique and bric-à-brac world. Yet this particular camera lens was causing him some agitation.

'Why doesn't he bloody well answer?' he said to Chrissie, his attractive, long-blonde-haired partner and co-host on the popular *Flotsam & Jetsam* TV show. 'I'm sure I can see him sitting watching us from behind those lace net curtains.'

'Shush, Fergie!' she whispered. 'You might be right, but it's hard to say from this distance. But if he's there then he'll be able to hear you on this intercom. Now don't swear.' She raised her hand to cover her eyes and looked admiringly up at the house. 'It's a fantastic place that he has here. And a fabulous view over his own stretch of beach.'

He straightened up from the stone pillar with the intercom and camera beside the radio-controlled iron gates that barred entry to the long drive. It zigzagged up through sand dunes to a large two-storeyed building that seemed to be more windows than brickwork. And all of them were covered with net curtains or blinds. He screwed his eyes up and pointed. 'Look, in that bay window. I'm sure he's sitting there watching us.'

'Maybe he only talks to people he recognizes?' she suggested.

He stared at her as if she had said something outrageous. 'In which case he's bound to recognize us, isn't he? Fergie and Chrissie from *Flotsam & Jetsam*. Half of Scotland watches us every night.'

'Maybe he's part of the other half of Scotland, my love.'

Despite himself he grinned at her. When Chrissie smiled like that men fell in love with her. When she smiled like that at him, he wanted to make love to her. He raised an eyebrow and flicked his eyes in the direction of the countless sand dunes that ran the length of the coast.

She immediately recognized the expression on his handsome, deeply tanned face and giggled. 'This is business, Fergie. Behave yourself. Now try again. They told us that he's just about a recluse and that we'd be lucky to get him to let us in.'

Fergie sighed and bent down to jab a well-manicured finger on the intercom button.

'Hi there,' he intoned in his jingle-jangle Scottish TV voice. 'This is Fergie and Chrissie here from *Flotsam & Jetsam*. We'd like to have a chat with you, maybe do a bit of business and invite you on to our TV show.'

'Maybe he's deaf, Fergie? Or maybe he's just not interested.'

'You look into the camera, darling. Maybe a sight of you will get him to open up.'

Chrissie gently barged him aside and smiled at the lens. But before she could say anything the intercom crackled and a distant tinny voice rang out.

'No hawkers, sales-folk or onion Johnnies, thank you.'

Fergie stared in disbelief. 'Hawkers! Onion Johnnies! Doesn't he know — ?'

The intercom crackled again. 'Please move on or I'll be telephoning the police.'

Fergie scowled and jabbed the button again. 'Now look here! I am Fergie Ferguson from the Scottish TV program *Flotsam & Jetsam* and I have — '

The voice from the intercom interrupted.

'Please move on. I do not like my privacy being invaded. I am phoning the police now.'

'Come on, Fergie,' said Chrissie, pointing to their parked Mercedes.

A motor engine sounded and they looked round to see a cream and blue mobile shop van that was also emblazoned with the logo of the Royal Mail appear round the bend of the rough track. It drew to a halt beside their car and a postman got out. He was a wiry fellow with a shaven head that made prominent ears stand out even more. He was wearing shorts and trainers and was almost as tanned as Fergie.

'Hello, folks,' he said with a grin. 'Are you trying to get to see our famous artist-cum-beachcomber? I have to say you'll be lucky.' Then his jaw dropped as he recognized the duo.

'Crikey! You are — er — Thingy and Chrissie, aren't you?' He snapped his fingers with embarrassment. 'I mean Fergie and Chrissie. The wife and I are planning to come and see the show tonight.'

'That's excellent,' Fergie replied with a show-biz smile that completely hid the chagrin he felt at being called *Thingy*. 'And we are trying to see Guthrie Lovat.'

'Without luck,' added Chrissie.

'He only really lets me and my wife in these

days,' the newcomer explained. 'I am Alec Anderson, by the way. I am the local postie and mobile-shop proprietor. You'll see me tootling all over the island at some stage or another.'

'Alec, do you think you could do us a favour?' Fergie asked, with an ingratiating grin. 'Could you get us in to see the old boy? We wondered if we could entice him on to the show, or maybe let us feature some of his work. It could be good for his business.'

Chrissie put a hand on Alec's arm. 'We could make it worth your while.'

Alec pursed his lips. 'That could be tricky. He's a cantankerous old so and so. Maybe I could put a word in though. It would be a matter of picking my time.'

'We are doing the show every night Monday to Friday this week and next,' Chrissie said. She gave him one of her presenter smiles. 'Is there anything that we could do to help you?'

A sparkle came into Alec Anderson's eye. Ever ready for a business opportunity he replied eagerly, 'The wife and I are dab hands at supplying refreshments at public meetings. If you like, we could have tea, coffee, rolls and sweets for your audience. Just like at the cinema.'

'No problem, Alec,' said Fergie with a

wink. 'You scratch our backs and we'll scratch yours. Just give Geordie Innes, our producer a ring.' He pulled out a card from his breast pocket and wrote a number on top.

'That's fine; I'll do that for you, Mr Ferguson. But maybe you could give me a day to sort it. He'll have been watching us and he'll be fair chuntering. He's a suspicious so and so and I'll need to let him get used to the idea.'

'It would be great to get him on the show,' Fergie went on. 'Celebrated local artist and all that. Good for West Uist too.' He produced a pair of sunglasses and put them on. 'So you have my card. Phone Geordie to arrange your refreshments, then Guthrie or you can phone me any time'

'You've been a great help, Alec,' said Chrissie, wrinkling her nose as she turned to go.

Her gesture seemed to have the desired effect, for Alec blushed.

He stood tapping the card against his teeth as he watched them get into the Mercedes and set off. He waved.

'But I think you'll be lucky to get Guthrie on TV,' he mused to himself as they disappeared round the bend of the track.

He pressed the intercom. 'It's Alec, Mr Lovat. I've brought your supplies and your post.'

He went back to his van and started up the engine. Then he pressed the zapper that opened the gates and once they had swung free he set off up the zig-zag drive.

'But who knows. Maybe the old goat would like to be a TV star. I think he would like that Chrissie.'

IV

Bruce McNab never really liked taking more than two clients out on the river at a time. For one thing it was hard enough trying to teach two people the intricacies of fly-fishing. And for another it was potentially unsafe, according to the faceless wonders in Health and Safety who were forever trying to put a stranglehold on folk such as himself. It was a continual worry whether the insurance company would pay up if anything did go wrong. Yet his main reason for keeping his numbers so small was because he was not one known to hold his tongue. If he thought someone was acting like a fool he would tell them, no matter how rich, powerful or titled that person might be. In his mind he was the expert on all types of hunting and game fishing and that was just the way it had to be. Give him three folk and he knew that there would be one clown among them.

In this trio of clients he just knew that there was an idiot of the first order. He just wasn't sure which of them it was.

'The skill is in the way that you make your fly react,' he said as he stood thigh deep in the waters of the Corlinspey River about fifty yards down from the Cauldron Pool. It was called that because the waters tumbled over a ledge at the edge of the Corlins into a foaming vortex before they cascaded down a series of mini rapids and the river meandered peacefully on. The three clients stood on the bank looking down at him each dressed in brand new sporting clothes and waders, with their rods at the ready.

'The trout is an intelligent fish. He has a good idea where he is going to get a tasty insect meal. He seems to know a real insect from a poorly disguised metal hook that is going to hoik him out of the water.' He turned and thrust out his bearded jaw challengingly. 'He will not be fooled by a galoot who fancies himself as a fisherman.'

He flicked his rod and cast his line at a deft forty-five degree angle to land in the Corlinspey.

'So you have to make it behave like a proper insect. You see? Easy!' He played the rod and line and this time didn't bother looking round. 'So what are you, gentlemen? Galoots or fishermen?' This time he turned and smiled, challenging them to either get cross or buckle down. He was in his early forties, but was proud of his physique, having kept himself in trim since his shinty-playing days. He had broad shoulders, a good-looking, well-weathered face with a full red beard and mane of hair. He looked every inch the gillie, and he was confident that he could handle himself with anybody if they decided to cut up rough. It had not yet happened in his career.

He grinned as he saw that all three were too busy wafting the air to fend off the odd midge.

'Och! I think you will find that I know how to fish well enough, Jimmie,' said the shortest of the three, a paunchy, middle-aged fellow with a Dundee accent. 'I have fished the length of the Tummel and the Tay.'

Bruce nodded, although he was not convinced. He tended to assess his clients on the basis of social status and sporting prowess. He had already tagged Dan Farquarson, a well-to-do businessman, as a B or a C grade.

'And what about you, Mr Thompson?' Bruce asked Dan Farquarson's associate. It was a rhetorical question as far as he was concerned, since he had already scored him as a low D or high E.

'I'm no so sure about my fishing ability, boss,' the man who had been introduced to him as Wee Hughie replied in a guttural Glaswegian brogue. It amused Bruce that Wee Hughie replied not to him, but to Farquarson. Clearly he was in thrall to the little man. Yet the epithet was not entirely right, for there was nothing obviously small about Wee Hughie Thompson. He was well over six feet in height and with the build of a weight-lifter. The image of the proverbial brick toilet sprang to Bruce McNab's mind.

'See, the only fishing I ever did was at the Glasgow Fair down on the Green. I wis about ten, I think. They gi'ed me a cane wi a loop and I had tae fish out a plastic duck from a rotating pond thing.'

Dan Farquarson made a throaty chuckle then immediately cursed as his hand went to scratch his thinning grey hair. 'You are a card, right enough, Hughie. Well I am betting that you'll catch a few bites today. Mind you they might just be midge bites, like these.'

'How about you just let us get in the river and we'll see how we do?' said the third member of the group with a flurry of impatience.

Bruce eyed him dispassionately. It was the

impatient tone of someone used to getting his own way. He had already recognized the long-blond-haired young man as none other than Sandy King, the Scottish footballer of whom all the newspapers were expecting great things from in the future. On that basis Bruce had already graded him as at least an A minus on his system.

'Be my guests,' he said, indicating for them to step down into the water. 'Take care of your first few steps. The water bed can be gie slippy and you do not want to fill your waders with water. I cannot stress that enough. It can be very dangerous.'

He stood back and watched them all get in. Then he pointed downriver. 'I suggest that you each select a spot twenty yards apart. That way you will be out of range of each other's cast and you will all get a decent shot at the fish.'

And indeed, with him wandering back and forth between them, giving little pointers according to their level of ability, they soon had two decent fish in their net. Dan Farquarson and the footballer had both surprised Bruce McNab.

Wee Hughie had been reprimanded three times, once by Dan Farquarson and once by Bruce for keeping up a flow of inane chatter. When he started to give them another commentary on how he was going to go for the big catch, Bruce determined to silence him.

'Mr Thompson,' he said, trying to relax so that his ire did not show too much. 'If you want to catch anything at all, you will need to keep quiet. Fish can see you and they can hear every — '

He did not finish because from the bank behind and above them someone started to laugh.

'Don't believe him, my friend. Fish don't have ears to hear with. Don't believe this gillie.'

They all looked round and were surprised to see a man in his mid-thirties dressed like them in waders, but with an anorak and a mesh helmet, such as bee-keepers wear. Hanging from a shoulder strap he was carrying a large box with numerous flasks and containers and in his free hand he had a huge gossamer net on a pole.

'Who do you think you are?' quipped Wee Hughie. 'A mad butterfly collector?'

'A mad scientist some say,' the man replied. 'Doctor Digby Dent, at your service.' He grinned behind the mesh of his helmet. 'And I am just about to join you gentlemen.'

'Not here, you aren't,' snapped Bruce. 'You have no licence to fish here.'

Digby Dent chuckled and tossed his net

down on the bank. Then he proceeded to clamber down into the water. 'And a good morning to you too — Mr McNab, isn't it?' Then before Bruce could reply, 'I have no need of a licence to retrieve my specimens. I have thirty traps embedded all the way along the bank here. It is time to collect them. They should give me a good idea of the midge larval population along this stretch of the river.'

Without more ado he started moving slowly along the river behind them, delving with his gloved hands into the muddy bank to locate and pull out a series of cone shaped plastic containers.

Sandy King noticed that there were small green tags embedded above each one.

'I think you should clear off, pal,' said Dan Farquarson. 'We have paid good money to fish this water and — '

'Then fish away,' replied Dr Dent. 'You won't disturb me.'

Bruce took a step towards him. 'Did you hear my client, Dent?'

'Oh yes, but I won't be long. I am conducting a serious scientific survey here, not kow-towing to the rich folk like you.'

'You should watch your mouth, pal,' said Dan Farquarson.

'Should I give him a ducking, boss?'

suggested Wee Hughie.

Dr Dent laughed again. 'Look, enough of your prattle. Just let me get on with my work then you can go back to your tiddler-catching, or whatever it is you are doing.'

'Are you the midge man that we heard about?' Sandy King asked.

Whether or not Dr Dent recognized the footballer, he gave no indication. He went on collecting his specimen containers, wiping the dirt off each one before adding it to the box.

'I am an entomologist, but to the folk round here that means I am the midge man. I am the chap who is going to free Scotland of the tyranny of the midge forever.'

'You are a fool, Dent,' sneered Bruce. 'The midges have been here long before man and they will be here long after we have gone.'

In the shade of the bank none of them had really seen the fine haze of the swarm that descended upon them. All the fishermen, including Bruce McNab started to itch and scratch and waft the air about them in a useless attempt to fend off their tiny attackers, which had honed in on them to bite and feed off blood.

'Bugger this for a lark!' exclaimed Dan Farquarson, the first to haul himself from the river. 'Let's get out of here before we're eaten alive. Why did you take us to this infested place?' he demanded of Bruce.

'It wasn't infested until he started guddling about in the bank,' Bruce replied, pointing venomously at Dr Dent.

'You should have checked up on the Midge Index. It is well displayed on the harbour noticeboard. It is high all week, which means that you should be prepared.'

'Midge Index! Rubbish!' Bruce exclaimed in disgust.

'Aye rubbish you say,' groaned Wee Hughie, pointing at Dr Dent's protective clothing. 'But he's prepared for it. Why are we not?'

Digby Dent grinned. 'A lot of the local folk think they know about the midges, just because they live alongside them. But the truth is that they don't, as your gillie has just proved.' He clicked his tongue then went on without looking up at them. 'Look, why don't you all come along to the *Flotsam & Jetsam* show tonight,' he said, as he casually went on with his specimen collecting. 'I am doing a few minutes on the life cycle of the midge. They want a bit of colour adding to their remarkable show,' he said, with a slight emphasis on the word 'remarkable.' Its subtlety was not lost on Sandy King. Then he grinned up at them. 'You really ought to dress properly when you go out on the river, you know. I could let you have the phone number of a good supplier of midge veils.'

'Come on,' Dan Farquarson said irritably. 'Why don't you find us another bit of the river where we won't be disturbed by these little buggers?' He looked sternly at Dr Dent. 'Or by any other nuisance.'

'Enjoy your sport,' Dr Dent called. 'I've enjoyed mine. If I had been along a bit earlier I could have netted that swarm. A pity that you broke it up like that.'

Bruce McNab's face had gone puce and he was about to reply, but thought better of it.

'You take care of yourself, pal,' said Wee Hughie, who had no such concerns. There was a snap as he stood on the long handle of the insect net. 'Whoops! Someone left a pole in my way.' He winked maliciously at Digby Dent who stood silently although it was clear that he had been rattled by the way his hands had begun to shake.

Sandy King gave a half smile. 'That sounds like good advice, Doctor Dent. And you know what they say — you should never bite off more than you can chew.'

V

Calum Steele the editor of the *West Uist Chronicle* had been working through the night to get the latest edition of his newspaper out on time. Since the paper was virtually a one-man show — Calum being not only the editor, but the sole reporter, manager and printer — it often meant that he had the devil's own job to write everything, prepare photographs and physically produce the newspaper in time for the fleet of lads he paid to distribute it to the newsagents and other outlets across the island.

Although he always talked about the *West Uist Chronicle* offices, it was a somewhat grandiloquent title, for although there was a large printed sign attached to the wall beside the door, the newspaper offices consisted of two floors, both of which were exclusively used by Calum. The actual news office itself, where Calum interviewed people and took orders for photographs which had appeared in the paper, occupied the first room on the ground floor, with an all-purpose junk room at the back. Before the days of digital photography it had been the dark room where he did his developing. Upstairs was where the actual work took place. At the front was the room with a cluttered old oak desk where he wrote his articles and columns on a vintage Mackintosh computer or on his spanking new laptop. Sitting between the two computers was a dusty old Remington typewriter, which served no real purpose other than to help him feel the part of a writer. The rest of the room was occupied with his digital printing press, paper and stationery supplies, and in the corner was the space where he stacked the next issue of the newspaper ready for distribution.

Across the landing was a larger room which had been divided up to form a kitchenette and a shower. The toilet was next door to that, and along from it was the archive room where all the past issues of the *Chronicle* were kept. On the landing there was room for a battered old settee and a camp-bed, which Calum used when he was either working late, or when he felt too inebriated to return home.

By the time the lads had arrived to take their piles of papers away that morning, Calum had consumed three bottles of Heather Ale and the better part of a half-bottle of Glen Corlin malt whisky. As a result he had paid the lads twice the usual amount and wished them a fond farewell before tumbling into the camp-bed intent upon sleeping until at least tea time.

He was only dimly aware of the downstairs bell ringing, a female voice calling out, then the sound of footsteps coming up the stairs.

'Mr Steele, I'm here! Where would you like me to start?'

Calum shoved the cushion away from his

face and propped himself up on an elbow and felt about on the floor for his wire-framed spectacles, without which he could barely see the end of his nose.

'What the . . . ? Who the blazes are you?'

He blinked several times and forced his bleary eyes to focus. As he did so he found himself looking at a pretty young woman in her early twenties with short crinkly hair and with large hoop ear-rings. She was dressed in jeans with fashionable holes in the knees, pink trainers and a T-shirt with the logo 'The West Uist Chronicle WRITES!'

'It's me, Cora Melville.'

'Cora? Melville?' A dim and worrying recollection was itching at the back of his mind.

Cora giggled. 'Of course, silly. You remember! My great-aunty introduced us at the ceilidh at New Year. I was just getting ready to do my last term in journalism at Abertay University and you and Great-aunt Bella arranged — '

'Bella Melville is your great-aunt?' Calum interrupted. He swallowed hard, for Miss Bella Melville had taught him and most of his friends on the island. All of them were still in awe of her.

Cora nodded enthusiastically. 'And so here I am, your new reporter ready to start my

36

new job.' She giggled again. An effervescent laugh that made him think of fizzy lemonade. 'So, where shall I start? I am so excited that you are going to teach me all about journalism.'

Calum's head began to throb. Now he remembered only too well. In a near drunken fit of magnanimity he had promised Miss Melville that he would employ Cora at the *West Uist Chronicle*.

'Ah, yes. I'm a wee bit tired just now, Cora. I need a bit of sleep. Why don't you — er — have a look round — quietly get to know the place.'

For a moment she looked a bit crestfallen. But it was only for a moment. She snapped her fingers. 'I know. A good reporter needs to know the style of the paper back to front. Is it all right if I look through your archives?'

Calum smiled. 'Aye, excellent idea. The archives are in the room back there. Help yourself. Read and digest. But quietly.' He yawned and screwed up his eyes to look at his watch. 'Give me a couple of hours then maybe you could make a cup of coffee. Strong black coffee.'

Cora smiled and clicked her heels, then saluted. 'Will do, sir. That will get you perky again. And it will give me time to familiarize myself with the past *Chronicle* stories.'

'That's the way, lassie. Just do it quietly, eh? I like your attitude. Good approach. A good journalist needs to be ever on the alert. Vigilance at all times.'

Cora giggled and skipped across the landing. 'Vigilance at all times, I like it. I'll make it my motto.'

'Aye, you do that,' Calum groaned as he slumped back on the camp-bed. He pulled the cushion over his face again. 'Vigilance at all . . . '

Within moments he was snoring gently away.

2

I

Sergeant Morag Driscoll was striding passed the multicoloured shop fronts of Harbour Street like a woman on a mission. She smiled at several of the merchants and traders as they set up their market-stalls along the sea wall in readiness for the inevitable market-day crowds. The harbour itself was crammed with a flotilla of yachts, fishing boats and motorboats, all bobbing up and down in the early morning sun. She had been off duty for a week and had recharged her batteries sufficiently to feel keen to get to the station to see how PC Ewan McPhee had managed in her absence. Under her arm she had a bag full of freshly baked butter rolls from Allardyce, the bakers and was looking forward to having one with a cup of Ewan's famous strong tea. It would be good to have five minutes to catch up before the locals started dropping in to lodge complaints, enquire about lost dogs, cats, budgies, or just to pass the time of day with whichever of the three regular members or the two special constables of the West Uist division of the Hebridean Constabulary was behind the desk.

A pretty, thirty-something, single mother of three, Morag fought a constant battle with herself. She was attractive by any standards, although she herself believed that she had a weight problem. It worried her and she worked hard to keep as trim as possible, since her husband had died unexpectedly from a heart attack when she was just twenty-six and she vowed that she would always be there for her children. On duty days her morning butter roll at the station was usually her first bite of the day, since she rarely had time to eat breakfast as she bustled about getting her kids up, fed and off to school. Although she felt guilty about the butter and what it might do to her cholesterol, one couldn't live without a little luxury now and then.

She stopped to look in the window of Staig's, the newsagents, as she walked, and thought that her reflection did not look too bad today. She was dressed in the blue Arran jumper with three small stripes on her arm to denote her rank, jeans and trainers. She turned slightly to the side and smiled as the side view confirmed her impression that she looked pretty trim. Slim enough to risk two butter rolls, maybe.

She scanned the posters in the window and the advertising cards sellotaped to the inside and noted the headlines on the framed *West Uist Chronicle* billboard in the entrance. She nodded to herself, pleased to see that nothing dire seemed to have happened while she was off.

'I'll have a *Chronicle* please, Willie,' she said as she entered the shop and handed over her loose change.

'Are you going to the *Flotsam & Jetsam* show this evening, Sergeant Driscoll?' asked Willie Staig, the bucolic-nosed newsagent. 'Should be good. The midge man is going to be on it.'

'Doctor Dent, the entomologist? What would he be doing on an antique show?'

'Bit of local colour, I am thinking. Since the news went out that they would be shooting the show here for the next fortnight the holidaymakers have come flooding in.' He grinned. 'And as they have come so it seems that the midges have brought their friends with them.' He leaned forward lest other customers should hear him. 'I have done a roaring trade in anti-midge creams and repellents. And as you and I know, none of them do very much at all.'

'Careful, Willie,' Morag said with mock sternness. 'That is bordering on an admission of a breach of the Trade Descriptions Act!'

She glanced up at the cardboard sign beside the old shop clock with its ancient advertisement for a famous type of snuff. 'I see it is a high Midge Index today. Good thing I am in the station all day.'

'Oh, that is you, is it, Morag Driscoll?' a familiar voice asked rhetorically from behind her. 'You have saved me the trouble of going up to the police station.

Morag grimaced at Willie Staig who fully understood her expression and kept a poker face. Morag turned round and found herself looking into the scrutiny of her old teacher's regard. She was a tall, silver-haired lady of about seventy, dressed in a tweed suit, swathed in a russet-coloured silk shawl. She had a handbag hanging from one arm and was pulling off one of her smart leather gloves as she regarded Morag.

'Why, Miss Melville, and what can I do for you on this fine day?'

'You can start by smiling, Morag Driscoll,' Bella Melville returned. 'I am sure you remember me telling you that many times when I was teaching you.'

Morag remembered only too well. Miss Melville had been the Kyleshiffin schoolteacher until her retirement and she had taught virtually half of West Uist's population. Few ever had

42

the temerity to argue with her and her opinions were well known and respected, if not always agreed with.

Morag forced a smile that she hoped was not too insipid for her old teacher's liking.

'That's better, Morag. You always were a serious girl and I always tried to make you relax, but . . . ' Miss Melville shrugged her shoulders as if to indicate that she had been a hopeless case. Then she smiled indulgently. 'But I suppose that is why you have become such an excellent police sergeant. Now,' she went on in her old no-nonsense manner, 'I really have an important request.' She frowned slightly. 'No, not a request, but a demand. The police will have to do something.'

'About what, Miss Melville?'

'Not *about* anything, Morag. Something will have to be done *for* Annie McConville.'

Morag said nothing, but nodded encouragingly.

'She is very upset about all these puppies and waifs.'

Morag frowned and was immediately rebuked.

'Don't beetle your brow like that, Morag. Don't you remember me telling you? The wind might change and you'll be left like it.' She sighed. 'I can see you are not following me. Well, that dog sanctuary of hers is just getting too much for her. She has had several abandoned puppies and a few strays to take in lately. And some cats. And they all seem to have been mistreated in some way or other. It simply is not good enough.' She unclasped her bag and drew out a purse.

'I — er — don't quite see how this concerns the West Uist Police, Miss Melville,' Morag said, with as expressionless a face as she could muster. 'Shouldn't you — '

'I should do exactly what I am doing, Sergeant Driscoll. I am reporting the whole thing to the police. Now it is up to you to investigate and sort this out.'

'But, but — '

Miss Melville looked at the bag under Morag's arm and smiled. 'Ah yes, your butter rolls. I expect Ewan McPhee and the Drummond boys will be waiting for their butteries.' She cocked her head to one side. 'But you just watch them, my lass. As they say, *Easy on the lips, heavy on the hips*! She reached over and picked up a copy of the *Chronicle* and laid down the exact change. 'There you go, Willie, and you just remember when you are writing your posters that *i comes before e, except after c*.' With which she tapped the news poster at the door and walked elegantly away, conscious of her own prim and sylph-like figure.

Morag and Willie gave each other a supportive smile. Miss Melville had the ability to make all of her former pupils feel like ten year olds again.

And Morag had lost her appetite for a hot butter roll.

II

The Kyleshiffin police station was a converted bungalow off Kirk Wynd, which ran parallel to Harbour Street. The walls were pebble-dashed and the garden had been tarmacked over to create a parking area complete with a bike rack and poles for tying dog leashes. Above the door was a round blue police sign and by the door was a glass-fronted case containing all sorts of information about things lost and found, and about various initiatives that had been made by the Hebridean Constabulary.

Inside the station, PC Ewan McPhee, the six foot four, freckled, red-haired wrestling and hammer-throwing champion of the Western Isles, and the junior officer of the West Uist division of the Hebridean Constabulary was having a difficult morning. It had started badly at six when he had gone for his usual early morning run up to the moor above Kyleshiffin where he could practise his hammer-throwing technique. He had won the Western Isles heavy hammer championship for five years in a row, breaking his own record on each occasion. He had even contemplated converting to throw the Olympic hammer, which demanded learning a whole new method; since the heavy hammer was done from a standing throw, as opposed to the whirling of the Olympic. He had been trying that out for about half an hour when the inevitable had happened.

A heather moor is not ideally suited to the rapid turns of the feet needed to build up pace to hurl the Olympic hammer and his feet got snagged in the purple heather just as he prepared to launch it. He felt himself falling and failed to release the great weight. As he landed heavily it swung over his head and landed with a great sucking noise in one of the pot bogs just feet away.

'Och, Ewan, you clumsy idiot!' he chastised himself. 'Never an Olympic thrower will you make.'

He sat up and was immediately aware that his hammer had disturbed a swarm of midges from the bog. Instantly, they were at him, biting him on all his exposed skin, which was mostly all over since he had stripped down to vest and shorts. Stopping only to pick up his track suit he beat a hasty retreat for the safety of Kyleshiffin police station. It was only when he was inside and enjoying the dubious comfort of a cold shower that he realized that he had left his precious hammer on the moor. He debated whether he would have time to go back for it before he forgot where the pot bog was that he had left it, but his mind was made up for him as he was in the process of dabbing himself dry and applying toothpaste to his numerous bites.

'Come on, come on!' a voice cried out from the hallway. Then a fist thudded a couple of times on the desk and Ewan pulled on his clothes and scuttled through to find one of his heart-sink regulars pacing back and forth on the other side of the desk.

It was Rab McNeish, the local carpenter and spare-time undertaker, a man who epitomized the word paradox. He was a tall, gaunt man with a stringy neck, yet he ate like a horse. At a funeral he was as silent as the grave itself, the perfect funeral director, yet with his carpenter's hat on he could be a foul-mouthed, bad-tempered and self-opinionated boor. He was almost bald, but had an up-and-over and had grown a drooping moustache in an attempt to compensate, but instead it all just gave him an even sourer look. That was

47

not helped by the fact that he was also one of life's great complainers.

One of Rab McNeish's greatest fears, which he often communicated to Ewan McPhee when he came complaining, was germs. This was understandable, since his younger brother had died ten years previously from toxoplasmosis.

'Those bloody dogs!' he said to Ewan, when he appeared behind the station counter. 'They are everywhere. And wherever they are, they poo and put everyone at risk of the pestilence that is toxoplasmosis.'

'What dogs are you meaning — ?' Ewan began.

'All of them, but especially all of them that Annie McConville keeps in that so-called sanctuary of hers. It is getting more and more crowded. They yap and yowl and create all manner of noise. I bet loads of the locals have been in complaining.'

'Er — no, I believe you are the first, Mr McNeish.' Ewan picked up a pen and opened the ledger to take notes. 'So, is it an official complaint that you are wanting to make?'

'A complaint? Me? About Miss McConville?' Rab McNeish looked scandalized. 'Not at all. I am just reporting how things are. It is my duty as a good citizen to report when I see loose poo around the place. And there is lots of it, let me tell you. There are dog waste bins all over, but are people using them?'

'Are you suggesting that Miss McConville is not using these bins?'

Rab shook his head in consternation and creased his brow. 'No! Leave Miss McConville out of this, will you? It's those incoming folk, I am betting. They come in their boats and their camper-vans and they let their dogs run wild. You'll have to do something about it.'

Ewan was starting to get flustered. He looked up from the ledger as the door opened and saw with relief Sergeant Morag Driscoll enter. His stomach responded to the smell of the hot rolls by gurgling.

'Ah, Sergeant Driscoll,' he said. 'Good to see you back. I was just listening to Mr McNeish here and he was telling me — '

'I was just reporting about all the dogs. They are everywhere, Sergeant. Everywhere!'

Morag pursed her lips. 'That is curious. Miss Melville was just talking to me about dogs. She was wanting us to do some investigating.'

Rab McNeish jabbed a finger in Ewan's direction. 'You see! You see?'

'But I don't see that it is a police problem,' Morag added.

Suddenly the door opened again and Inspector Torquil McKinnon rushed in, his Cromwell helmet under one arm and the

Bullet's panniers over the other. His bagpipes protruded from one and the bedraggled floppy head of a mongrel dog from the other.

'Can't stop, folks,' he said, as he ducked under the counter flap, heading for his office. 'I've got a sick dog here.'

Rab McNeish took a step backwards. 'Sick, did he say?' Then, jabbing the air at both Ewan and Morag he quickly retreated to the door. 'Ugh! Mark my words, I told you so. We've got a problem on the island.'

Ewan stood scratching his head as the door swung to behind the undertaker.

'You look as if you've been half bitten to death, Ewan,' Morag observed. 'What is it? Midges?'

'Aye. But speaking of biting, are those butteries up for grabs?'

Morag was still reeling from her encounter with Miss Melville and her parting remark. With a sigh she handed them over. 'They are all for you, my wee darling. Now what say you make us all a cup of your best tea and let's see what the boss has just brought in.'

III

Torquil placed the panniers on the easy chair beside his desk then gingerly lifted the dog out. It was shivering and its teeth were chattering. He lay it down on the floor and it whimpered, before weakly licking his hand once.

'You poor wee fellow. You look exhausted.'

He fetched a towel and, as gently as he could, he tried to give it a rub down.

Morag tapped on the door then let herself in. 'Tea and a buttery is on its way, Torquil.' Her eye fell on the puppy and she smiled. 'What a bonny wee dog. Where did you find him? He looks as if he's been swimming.'

Torquil told her of finding the animal tied to a piece of timber.

'It was lucky for him that I came along. I reckon he would either have died between now and the next tide, or it would have taken him out again and then he would have been done for.'

'So someone was trying to get rid of him?' Morag asked in disbelief as she squatted down to stroke the dog. 'How cruel can anyone get? Why he's little more than a puppy.'

'That's what it looks like. And I just hate cruelty to animals.'

'So what are you going to do?'

'We'll put a poster up and maybe ask Calum Steele to put something in the *West Uist Chronicle*. If someone claims him, and they can convince me that they didn't try to drown him, then they can have him back.'

He opened the door in answer to Ewan McPhee's gentle kick on the door frame. 'Ah, a buttery. Thanks, Ewan.' He took a roll and a mug of tea and sipped his tea. 'But I suspect that no one will show up.'

Ewan bent and patted the dog. 'I heard what you were saying, boss. So what are you going to do with him now? Should I phone Annie McConville and see if she'll take him in?'

Morag sucked air between her lips. 'Actually, I don't think that's a good idea. Miss Melville collared me in Staigs and told me that she's inundated with strays. She wants us to do something about it.'

Torquil groaned. 'Us? What does she expect us to do?' He looked at his colleagues who both shrugged. 'Then I guess we'll have to just hold on to him for now. We'll see if we can't get him back on his paws.' He nibbled his roll. 'We'd better get some dog food in, Ewan.'

'I'll go and get some right away, boss. But would it be OK if I popped up to the moor? I sort of left my hammer up there.'

Torquil grinned as the big constable explained. 'Aye, go on, Ewan. And while you're getting the dog food, see about a collar and a lead. You never know, before long you might be taking him up to the moor for a regular walk.'

The outside bell rang, indicating that the front door had opened. There was the sound of heavy boots outside. Ewan took a step towards the door, but stopped with his hand on the handle.

'Does that mean we'll be keeping him here, boss? A station dog?'

The office door opened and a peal of synchronous laughter rang out. Two tall men, both even taller than Ewan, dressed in fishermen's oilskins and wearing bobble hats came in. It was the Drummond twins, Douglas and Wallace. They were as identical as identical twins can be.

'A station dog!' Douglas exclaimed.

'Ah, our two special constables,' said Ewan with a half smile, theatrically looking at his watch. 'Good of you to drop in. How was your fishing?'

'Good enough, thank you, PC McPhee,' said Wallace.

'But stop evading the question, Ewan McPhee,' said Douglas. 'Did you just say that this was the new station dog?' He pursed his lips as he looked down at the forlorn looking animal. 'Is it the runt of the litter?'

Torquil explained how he had found the

dog. He scratched its head, eliciting another whimper, then a turn of the head and another feeble lick on the hand. 'Since we do not know his name, until further notice to the contrary, I propose to call him Crusoe.'

'After Robinson?' Morag queried, with a smile. 'You do that Inspector McKinnon, but could the station sergeant ask a simple question — where is he going to stay at night? Here on his own at the station? I only ask because if you are thinking that we can share his care out between us, as we do the night duty, I can't offer to take him home because of my Jim's asthma. He reacts to dog fur.'

Ewan shuffled his size fourteen feet. 'And I am afraid that my mother won't have another dog in the house since our old Labrador died.'

'Don't look at us; we have enough trouble looking after ourselves,' said Wallace.

'To say nothing of our unwholesome habits,' added Douglas.

Torquil grinned. 'Then it looks as if he'll be coming home to the manse to stay with the Padre and me.'

Morag raised a quizzical eyebrow. 'Are you sure that Lachlan won't mind? And what about Lorna? Will she be happy about you having a dog?'

Torquil was not sure how to answer either

question. He and his uncle had always enjoyed a close and easy relationship together. They had so many shared interests; the bagpipes, fishing, golf and building and riding their classic motorcycles. He was pretty sure that he would be quite relaxed about Crusoe's temporary residence at the St Ninian's manse.

Lorna Golspie his girlfriend might not be so happy, of course. The problem was that he could not ask her right away since Superintendent Lumsden, his superior officer had quite deliberately seconded her to the office on Lewis as special liaison officer with the Customs. That meant that they were only able to communicate by mobiles and only saw each other one weekend in three. He knew that today she would be unavailable until the evening.

'I'll take a chance on them both,' he said.

Curiously, as if he had understood the conversation that had been going on, Crusoe raised his head and gave a feeble bark. Then he wagged his tail against the floor.

'Looks like it is a done deal, boss,' said Wallace Drummond.

Then, almost immediately, Crusoe's ears pricked up and he raised his head again to give three quick forceful barks. Then he wagged his tail again before lying down and closing his eyes.

'Poor thing is shattered,' Torquil mused. 'Ewan, maybe you better go and get that food for Crusoe. And then go and find your hammer.'

IV

Calum Steele had been in love with Kirstie Macroon, the anchor person of the Scottish TV early evening news and light entertainment programmes, ever since he first saw her. On many occasions he had provided her with news features and occasionally had been interviewed by her on the news slot. He had been devastated to learn that she had been engaged to a TV reporter by the name of Finbar Donleavy[1], but had hoped that when Donleavy was offered a position with CNN in America that the relationship might falter. When he lifted the telephone and heard her voice he felt his heart start to race. And when she started telling him how much she cared for him he felt as though he was floating on cloud nine.

'Calum!' someone shouted. 'Calum!'

Calum shot bolt upright in his camp-bed, instantly realizing with dismay that the voice

---

[1] See *Murder Solstice*.

that had called his name was not that of Kirstie Macroon. He looked desperately to right and left as if the act of looking would somehow conjure her up.

'Och, it was just a dream!' he sighed.

'Calum! I mean, Mr Steele,' came the voice again, but this time it was clearly coming from the archives room.

'Who's that?' he asked, rubbing his eyes blearily.

'You are a genius,' said Cora Melville, appearing in the doorway with a stack of old *Chronicles* in her arms. 'I hadn't realized what a brilliant newspaper you run here all by yourself. I had only seen it once or twice when I came over to West Uist to visit my Great-aunt Bella and, as a kid, I wasn't really into papers, but now ... ?' She sighed admiringly. 'It is fantastic. I can't get over how meticulously you have chronicled every-thing in the *Chronicle*.' Then, finding what she had said to be hilarious, she jack-knifed forward and let out a belly-laugh that ended in an effervescent giggle. 'Chronicled in the *Chronicle*, that's hilarious.'

Calum eyed her suspiciously. 'Are you on something, lassie?'

Cora pulled herself together. 'Just enthusi-asm, Mr Steele. And I do think you are a genius.'

'A genius, eh?' he repeated, permitting himself a little smile of pride. 'Why is that, lassie?'

'I just love your rustic style of writing. It is very simple so that anyone would understand what you are saying. But your versatility and your enthusiasm show through all the time.' She slapped a hand on the pile of old papers. 'It doesn't matter whether you are talking about the price of herring roe, covering a murder, or writing about finding a body in the loch, you make it sound the most important thing in the world.'

'A journalist has to be passionate — er — Cora, isn't it?'

She nodded. 'But I would just like to see some of the stories finished off. I have been reading back over the past year and it has been like reading a soap, a bit like 'The Archers' on the radio. I feel I know so many of the West Uist folk now.'

Calum swung his feet over the side, yawned and drew himself up to his full five foot six inches. 'What time is it? And what do you mean by finishing the stories off?'

'It's eleven o'clock, Mr Steele. And I mean that some of the stories seem headline news for an issue or two and then just disappear when I wanted to know what happened.'

'You can call me Calum, Cora. Everybody

does.' He grunted. 'Or most people do unless I rub them up the wrong way. Then they either call me Steele, or worse!' He shrugged nonchalantly. 'And that is the way of the news. Stories do just peter out. The art of journalism is to have something else to write about, and to be just as passionate about.'

Cora was staring at him with, large, brown doe-eyes. 'I just know that I am going to learn so much from you, Calum. So where shall I start? Can I have a big story to cover, like this?'

She held up the top paper with the headline THE BLONDE IN THE LAKE. 'You see, this is one of the stories I was talking about. It is so interesting. This woman found naked, floating face down in Loch Hynish. You covered it for several issues, then nothing.'

Calum stroked his chin. 'Ah yes, that was almost exactly a year ago. McQueen was her name. She was a PhD student working with Doctor Dent, the midge man. It looks as if she had just gone for a midnight swim in the loch, or something, and got into trouble and drowned. They found alcohol and drugs in her system, you see. She probably just swam out of her depth and got into trouble. Death by Misadventure the Fatal Accident Inquiry concluded.'

'But what happened to her? Where was she buried?'

'Here on West Uist. In the St Ninian's cemetery. Apparently she was alone in the world and loved the island. Strange though, no one except Doctor Dent showed up for her funeral.'

Cora stared at him in horror. 'But that's awful. How could people be so callous?'

'Rule one of journalism, Cora: only be judgmental if it will sell newspapers.' He yawned again and scratched his ample belly, as he was wont to do regardless of company. 'As for what sort of thing we'll have you doing, well, we'll just have to see what comes in. In the meanwhile, a good cub reporter has to know how to make good tea. I like mine fawn coloured and with four sugars.'

Cora was busy making the tea when the telephone rang and Calum answered it. She heard him talking into the receiver and scratching away on a scribbling block.

'Fascinating! Aye, of course I'll come. In fact, I'll be bringing my assistant to show her the ropes. Righto then, see you in ten minutes.'

Cora entered with a mug of tea in each hand, in time to see Calum pull on shoes and reach for a grubby yellow anorak that hung behind the door.

'There is serendipity for you,' he said, grabbing a motorcycle helmet. 'No rest for the wicked and certainly no time for tea. There's a whale beached at Largo Head. We'll need to scoot. Have you got transport?'

'I've got my mountain bike.'

Calum pointed to his spare helmet. 'That's not going to be fast enough. Have you ever ridden on the back of a Lambretta?'

'I've never even heard of one,' Cora replied with a grin.

'If that was a joke then we'll get on fine,' Calum replied. 'Either way, you're in for a treat. And a scoop! We'll probably make the nationals with this — maybe even Scottish TV.' And, as he immediately thought of Kirstie Macroon, he smiled bashfully. 'Come on, we've a story to cover.'

V

After golf Lachlan and Kenneth had popped into the church to say morning prayers together, then they had gone back to the manse for tea and toast. Kenneth had dutifully paid his debt of five pounds; much to his chagrin, but to Lachlan's diplomatically concealed satisfaction.

'Now tell me,' Lachlan said, as he sat back

and filled his briar pipe from his oilskin pouch. 'Why did the mere mention of Doctor Digby Dent's name make you lose the match? You pretty well had me against the ropes and you had a good chance of taking my money. I recognized the signs of pent-up fury, Kenneth.'

The Reverend Kenneth Canfield returned Lachlan's questioning gaze with a look of steely defiance. But in a moment the look disappeared and he let out a sigh of resignation.

'I cannot help it, Lachlan. I just cannot forgive the man.'

The Padre tamped the tobacco down in his pipe, but desisted from lighting it. It sounded as if Kenneth was on the point of unburdening himself.

'You cannot forgive him for what, Kenneth?'

'For the death of a beautiful young woman,' Kenneth said, quickly picking up his tea and taking a good sip. He sucked air between his teeth and gave a wan smile. 'I don't suppose you have a decent whisky in the manse, have you, Lachlan?'

Lachlan beamed and heaved himself out of his chair. 'Funny you should ask that, Kenneth. It just so happens I have a fine bottle of twenty-five year old Glen Corlan.'

VI

Torquil was sifting through papers while Crusoe lay by his feet, slumbering contentedly after having eaten the better part of a large tin of dog food and lapped up a bowl of water. A commotion had been going on in the outer office and he was listening to it with half an ear.

'It is a disgrace!' a man's voice cried out, despite Morag's calm remonstrations.

'I want to see the organ grinder, not his monkey!'

Torquil looked up and sucked air in between his lips. That would be bound to make Morag's hackles rise. That was never a good thing to do, for she could take good care of herself. He smiled and returned his attention to the reports in front of him.

He was surprised to hear Morag's tap on the door a few moments later.

'Sorry to bother you with this, Torquil,' she said, slipping into his office and closing the door behind her. He could not help but notice the broad grin on her face. 'This will amuse you,' she whispered. 'It is that Doctor Digby Dent and he's seething.' She put a hand to her mouth to suppress a laugh that threatened to erupt.

'The entomologist? What's the problem?'

'Someone has broken his midge net.' This time she could not contain a snigger.

Torquil raised his shoulders. 'Why is that funny?'

'He says it was done by a gang. And one of them was Sandy King.' She took a deep breath and repeated emphatically, '*the* Sandy King!'

'The footballer?'

Morag nodded enthusiastically. 'Aye, himself! Now do you see why it's so funny? You know his nickname, don't you? He's called The Net-breaker on account of his left foot.'

Torquil grinned. 'You and your football, eh, Morag.'

His sergeant's eyes widened. 'Come on, Torquil. Sandy King isn't just any footballer. He's played in Europe and also for Motherwell and Hamilton Academicals. There's talk of him maybe moving to play for The Picts. He's a certainty for the next international.'

Torquil nodded, wary of getting Morag going on about football. 'So what is he doing breaking our noted entomologist's insect net here on West Uist?'

Morag shrugged. 'Search me, but I thought maybe you should have a word with the midge man. Maybe say that we will investigate it. It would sound good coming from you.' She looked at her nails, then said casually, 'Then maybe send me to interview Sandy King.'

Crusoe whimpered in his sleep then rolled over and started snoring gently. Torquil grinned at him, then at Morag. He got up and came round his desk.

'OK, so now I see the ulterior motive. Lead the way.'

Digby Dent was a handsome man with olive skin and dark hair. His only marring feature was a surly turn of his mouth. Standing in his waders and full protective clothing, with his insect visor hanging down his back he presented a slightly comedic figure holding the two halves of his broken insect net.

'It was a deliberate act of vandalism,' he said, without waiting for pleasantries. 'That ruffian McNab and his cronies did this. One of them was some sort of footballer, I think. King, or something like that. Do you have any idea how much these things cost? The net is as thin as gossamer, it's the finest netting you can get, which is what I need to catch a swarm of insects.'

Torquil listened as he described the whole encounter while Morag took notes.

'And you want us to investigate this?' Torquil asked.

'I do, and I want to press charges.'

Torquil looked doubtful. 'It may just end

up as your word against theirs. And you say that there were three of them?'

Dent looked taken aback. 'But I don't care how many of them there were. I am telling you how it was. I am an academic at the University of the Highlands. Damn it, Inspector McKinnon, you know me.'

Torquil forced a genial smile to his lips. 'Aye, I know you, Doctor Dent,' he replied affably. 'And I am going to put Sergeant Driscoll here on to the case straight away. We shall see what her investigation turns up, shall we?'

Dr Dent looked unimpressed. 'Justice! That's all I want. Justice.'

Morag smiled at him. 'We'll see what we can do, Doctor Dent.'

VII

After delivering the dog food and a new leash at the station, Ewan had retraced his way to the moor above Kyleshiffin. Ever vigilant, a maxim that Torquil, his inspector and friend, was forever drumming into him, he had noticed a near bald tyre on a canary-yellow camper-van that was parked just off the road out of town, just before the bend where the track leading up to the moor started.

Although he had lived on the island all his life he never tired of the smell of the moor, with its heather, moss and the unmistakable fragrance of the peat. As he approached it he took a great gulp of air and broke into a jog.

He had a good idea of where his hammer had landed and he had been bitten by the midges. Fortunately, now that it was mid-morning there would be none around and so it would be safe to have a good poke about. He blinked as he saw a sparkle, like the glint of sun off glass in the heather in the direction that he was running. It disappeared as quickly as it had come and he jogged on.

'Oh please, Lord, don't let my hammer sink into the bog,' he mused to himself. 'It would be like losing my best friend.'

Then he saw the glint again, but this time he realized that there were actually two glints, like the reflection off a pair of binoculars.

'Hello!' he called out. 'If there is anyone there, have you seen a hammer?'

His question had the desired effect, albeit not immediately. A head popped up from the heather. Then another rose beside it. Then two figures climbed to their feet as he jogged up to them.

'What the heck do you think you are doing?' demanded one of the men.

Ewan jogged to a stop in front of them.

They were both wearing bobble hats, camouflage gear and green Wellington boots. He did not like the sullen look of the man who had just spoken. He was a swarthy, stocky man of about thirty with a gold ear-ring in one ear.

'West Uist Police,' Ewan said. 'PC McPhee here.'

Both men seemed to stiffen slightly. Then they glanced shiftily at each other.

'Police? What's the problem, Officer?' said the other man, a lean, unshaven fellow in his mid-twenties. 'We're just bird-watching.'

His companion was not so affable. 'And do you realize that you've probably trodden on that nest. You've probably killed all three of those red-crested moorhammer chicks.'

'I don't think I trod on any nest,' Ewan replied, maintaining his natural friendliness. 'But as I asked, have either of you seen a hammer near here? A highland throwing hammer.'

The lean man smiled and reached down into the heather. 'You must mean this. I thought it was an old cannon ball tied to a post.'

'That's my hammer, right enough,' Ewan said taking it gratefully. 'It's a beauty and I wouldn't like to be without it. I'll let you get on with your bird-watching then.' He turned to go then turned back. 'Are you the owners of a yellow camper-van parked down the road?'

'We are. We are here for the wildlife, and it is full of all our cameras and telescopes. There's nothing wrong is there? I thought it was OK to park there,' the lean one said.

Ewan shook his head. 'It's OK parked there, but the off side rear tyre is getting a bit bare. You should see to that straight away. It is illegal as it is.'

'We'll deal with it straight away,' the surly, stocky chap assured him.

Ewan nodded then left, taking a slightly circuitous route to avoid the line of the nest. But, as he headed down the track, he started wondering. He was not entirely sure that they had been watching the moor itself. From where they were, they could have been watching something or someone down in Kyleshiffin.

And he was not sure that he had ever heard of a red-crested moorhammer.

3

I

Calum had dashed up the stairs of the *Chronicle* offices upon finding that the front door had been forced open in their absence.

'The beggars!' he cried, as Cora darted up and joined him on the landing.

In every direction it was chaos. Piles of old newspapers had been cast everywhere. The camp-bed had been tipped over and the desk had been swept of everything except the heavy old Remington typewriter.

'Who would do something like this?' Cora asked.

'The same folk who sent us on that wild goose chase to Largo Head,' Calum replied sourly. 'They dragged us away so that they could give the place the once over.' He pulled out a handkerchief and gingerly pulled open the top drawer of a large grey filing cabinet. He grunted as he saw that his Glen Corlan whisky was still there, as was his old sporran in which he kept the petty cash. He stood looking round then shook his head. 'No, nothing has been taken. It was just a bit of wanton damage.'

Cora patted him on the shoulder. 'Don't worry, Calum,' she said in as cheery a voice as she could muster up. 'I'll have it ship-shape in no time.' With which she bent down to start gathering the discarded newspapers.

But Calum grabbed her shoulder and stopped her. 'Touch nothing, Cora!' he ordered. 'Whoever did this meant it as a serious message, believe me.' He tapped the side of his nose. 'When you've been a newsman as long as me you get an instinct for these things. We'll need to get the police round. I'll give my old mate Torquil McKinnon a bell in a minute.'

He reached into a voluminous pocket of his anorak and produced a small digital camera. 'But before I do, I'll just take a few pictures of the crime scene.'

'For the police?' Cora asked.

Calum shook his head. 'No lass. For the *Chronicle*. I'll write a piece straight away and it'll go in the next edition. Always remember that the pen is mightier than the sword.'

Cora nodded appreciatively. 'You are so right, Calum. You can humiliate them in print.'

The little newspaper editor shrugged his shoulders. 'Maybe, but I bet they'll just have a good laugh.' He shook his head and his jaw muscles tightened. 'Perhaps I didn't mean that exactly, about the pen being mightier than the sword. It would be more satisfying to

71

shove a pen up their noses when I get hold of them.'

Alec Anderson drove his mobile shop-cum-Royal Mail van into the parking bay at the front of his shop at the end of Harbour Street. Like the van, the shop-front was painted cream and blue with a Royal Mail red canopy shading and sheltering the crates of fruit and vegetables, and the assortment of fishing rods, nets, beach balls, whirly-windmills and umbrellas that proclaimed that Anderson's Emporium sold most of the things you would need on a West Uist holiday. To emphasize that, on one side of the door was a man-size figure of a kilted highlander licking an ice cream. This last accoutrement had been in the Anderson family's posses-sion, as had the shop, for three generations, although in recent years Alec had replaced the pipe the highlander had smoked for fifty years with a facsimile of the large ice creams that his emporium was famous for.

At his signature tune peep on the horn — a snatch of a hornpipe — a pretty auburn-haired woman popped out.

'Hello, my wee darling Agnes,' he called,

jumping out of the van and hauling his mail bag after him.

'Welcome home, love-bug,' she replied, skipping to meet him and planting a big kiss on his cheek.

An elderly lady dressed in a cheesecloth dress with an ill-fitting panama hat, with a prodigiously large shoulder bag was just tying the leads of five dogs to a large ring in the wall. 'Oh heavens! Don't look, Zimba, Sheila and you young ones,' she said, good-humouredly addressing a disdainful German shepherd, a zestful West Highland terrier and three boisterous collies. 'The Andersons' behaviour is enough to put me off my food, let alone you lot! Now, just you all keep your wheesht while I do my purchasing.'

She straightened and swung her shoulder bag into a more comfortable position, then she shook her head at the grinning couple who stood arm in arm regarding her with a mixture of amusement and embarrassment.

'Och, we are sorry to offend you, Mrs McConville. I haven't seen Alec for a few hours and I just miss him when he isn't here.'

'As I do you, Agnes, my love.'

Annie McConville glanced heavenwards. 'It is twenty years since I was widowed, but I cannot remember the lovey-dovey stuff lasting more than a few months, not how ever

73

many years you two have been together. It isn't natural, I am thinking.'

'Seven years,' Alec sighed. 'And it is perfectly natural, Annie, I assure you. Natural for us at any rate. And we don't mind showing our feelings.'

Annie gave a shudder then led the way into the shop. 'Well, let me bring you down from your cloud and do business.' She pointed to the shelf of pet food. 'I will be needing three times my usual order of Shepherd's Best for my hungry crowd. I have a dozen more at the moment and the number seems to be going up. It is criminal the way folk just abandon these poor creatures.'

Agnes went behind the counter and reached up for two double packs of dog food. She stacked them on the counter, then added another on top. 'That is just what PC Ewan McPhee was saying a few minutes ago. He said that Torquil McKinnon brought a stray in this morning.'

Annie gave a plaintive sigh. 'Oh deary me, that may be another wee doggie for my sanctuary I suppose.'

Agnes took Annie's capacious shoulder bag and started loading it with the packs of Shepherd's Best. 'That's going to be pretty heavy, I am afraid,' she said. Then she smiled as Annie gave her the stern look of an independent woman. 'But actually, Ewan gave me the impression that they plan to keep the dog. It sounds as if they have all taken to it at the police station.'

She shifted her glance from Annie's bag to Alec's mail bag. He had been standing listening to their exchange. 'Whatever have you been doing this morning? That bag seems fuller than when you went on your round. You are supposed to deliver the mail you know.'

Her husband laughed. 'As the Kyleshiffin sub-postmaster my job is to collect the mail as well as deliver it, as you well know, my heather bunch. And this collection is almost entirely from Guthrie Lovat — which you will already have guessed. It is his weekly postbag of things to all parts of the world.'

'Guthrie Lovat the beachcomber?' Annie asked. 'Sure, he must be about your best customer — or client, as I expect you call him these days.'

Alec grinned. 'He is a good customer, right enough. We seem to send his work to just about every corner of the world.'

'Aye he seems to be quite the famous artist these days,' replied Annie. 'Or what some folk call art, at any rate. But I remember him when he was just plain Guthrie Lovat, the beachcomber, scraping a living by selling all the flotsam and jetsam that got washed up on the West Uist beaches. Then he found that some of the tourists liked some of the bits and pieces he carved, or stuck together, and he started getting commissions. He'd never even been to art school, but somehow he built up a reputation and made a parcel of money. Enough to buy the strip of beach at Half Moon Cove.'

Alec laughed. 'Aye, he's a proper millionaire now. A regular Howard Hughes. I am guessing that me and Agnes are about the only folk he lets into the Crow's Nest.'

He gave them both a knowing wink. 'Except tomorrow he's letting VIPs in to see him and his work.'

Agnes was leaning forward on the counter. 'Go on then, tell us. What VIPs?'

'He has agreed to let Fergie Ferguson and Chrissie from the TV show *Flotsam & Jetsam* in to interview him. And then he's going on their show.'

'You are kidding!' Agnes exclaimed.

'Gospel, so help me,' Alec replied. He told them of his meeting at the gates of the Crow's Nest.

'So I gave him their card when I went in to pick up all this stuff and he even got me to phone them up. It must be a first. I don't think he's ever done an interview since Calum Steele did one in the *West Uist*

Chronicle a few years ago.'

Annie clicked her tongue. 'Aye and that was a hatchet job. Our Calum knows how to make enemies.'

'Anyway, he seemed to like the idea. I guess he feels it could do his business a bit of good.' He stopped and grinned. 'From what he said he doesn't think that they are *real* people.'

At which all three of them laughed.

'Some people seem happy today. Is it a private joke?' came Dr Dent's voice. He had entered the shop unnoticed, despite the fact that he was still wearing his waders. He stood with his broken insect net in one hand and with his specimen collecting box hanging from one shoulder.

'Good morning, Doctor Dent,' said Alec. 'I don't suppose there is any harm in telling, since it will be on TV soon enough. Guthrie Lovat has agreed to let the *Flotsam & Jetsam* folk see him. He got me to phone Fergie Ferguson while I was delivering his mail. And I have to say that Fergie seemed right pleased.'

'Interesting,' returned Dr Dent. 'I could do with seeing him myself. I've tried telephoning, but the last time I spoke to him he just said there was no way he would have me on his land.' He shrugged. 'The Lord only knows why.'

Annie McConville frowned. 'Oh he is such a rude scunner. Always was.'

'I have got a pretty good idea about the insect population of West Uist,' went on Dr Dent, 'but I have an idea that the Half Moon Cove area could be very different to the rest of the island. You see, it's like a funnel to the Atlantic Ocean, I believe that knowing more about the midge larval population around the beach and the sand dunes could be very interesting scientifically. That is why — '

'Why don't you make a plea on the *Flotsam & Jetsam* show tonight?' Annie suggested. 'I see that you are going to be on the programme already.'

Dent nodded, and then looked at Alec. 'I hadn't thought of that. But then I hadn't heard this news about Guthrie Lovat. I will do just that. But perhaps if Alec here also had a quiet word in Mr Lovat's ear, it would help to get me in through that barbed wire fence of his.'

Alec considered for a moment then nodded in agreement. 'Anything I can do to help the progress of science.' He pointed to Dr Dent's insect net. 'Have you had an accident with your midge net there?'

The entomologist told them of his encounter at the river and about reporting the incident to the police.

'Why not let Calum Steele at the *West Uist Chronicle* know about it as well?' Agnes suggested. 'He is always on the lookout for news. That would be right up his street.'

'Hmm, maybe,' Dr Dent grunted. 'Though he has a tendency to distort things, as I know through experience.' He shrugged as if dismissing the matter. 'Meanwhile I'll need some of your finest fishing line to see if I can mend the net.'

Agnes nodded. 'I'll be with you as soon as I have finished with Mrs McConville.'

'Ah, you'll be wanting money then,' Annie said to her. Then she took a sharp intake of breath when Agnes told her the price. 'Goodness, I'll be needing a bank loan soon.'

'Ha! Everything is so expensive these days, isn't it?' Dr Dent said. He turned to Alec and pointed to the post office counter at the end of the shop. 'So I think I had better draw some money out of my account while I am here. A new insect net like that will be expensive to replace and I can't be without something. I will need to send to the mainland for another.'

Alec nodded with his usual cheerfulness. 'Let me just deal with my bag and then I'll see to your money.'

'Oh yes, and I'll take a bottle of your best malt whisky, too,' Dr Dent added. 'I might need a bit of Dutch courage before this TV show.'

III

Morag pushed open the door of the Bonnie Prince Charlie Tavern on Harbour Street and weaved her way through the lunchtime crowd.

Mollie McFadden the doughty landlady of almost sixty years was pulling a pint with well-practised ease as she marshalled her staff as they bustled about with trays of tantalizing smelling seafood and pints of Heather Ale. She peered at Morag through her pebble-thick spectacles and gave her a broad smile as she recognized her.

'Why Sergeant Driscoll, it is not often that we have the pleasure of your company at lunchtime.' She placed the pint before a thirsty customer and collected his money with a smile.

'And what can I be getting you, Morag? Are you here for the celebration? A birthday maybe? Or to meet a gentleman?' Her eyes twinkled mischievously and she raised a hand to push her spectacles back on her nose, revealing as she did so a well-developed forearm, a consequence of having pumped a veritable sea of the Bonnie Prince Charlie's own Heather Ale over the years.

'No such luck,' Morag returned with a down-turned mouth. 'Just police business.'

'No trouble, I hope?' Mollie asked, a trace of anxiety flashing behind her spectacles.

Morag shook her head with a grin. 'Nothing like that. I am trying to track down a fishing party who were out with Bruce McNab this morning.'

Mollie's face brightened. 'Oh they are in the Prince's Suite at this very minute. They wanted a bit of privacy you see. One of them is a chap who doesn't believe in wallets. He's a tubby wee Dundonian chap I think. Some sort of big business chappie. He just pulled out a roll of twenties and peeled the notes off like he was tossing a lettuce salad. They all came in dribs and drabs.' She eyed Morag suspiciously. 'There is nothing dodgy about them, is there? I wouldn't like to see them sucking Bruce McNab into anything illegal.'

'Don't worry, Mollie, I am sure it will all be fine. I just need to have a chat with them.' She pursed her lips and leaned forward conspiratorially. 'Did you notice if Sandy was one of them?'

'Sandy who?'

'Sandy King, the footballer!'

Mollie shrugged unconcernedly. 'No idea. I

don't follow the football. I prefer my men to play a hardier game than that. Something like shinty.' Her eyes seemed to grow misty behind the thick lenses. 'Like Bruce McNab. Now he really was a shinty player to watch.'

Morag made her way past the portrait of Bonnie Prince Charlie to the Prince's Suite and noticed that the 'Reserved, Do not Disturb' sign was stuck to the glass panel of the door. She ignored the message, rapped twice on the wood and immediately entered.

'Excuse the interruption, gentlemen,' she said. 'I am Sergeant Morag Driscoll of the West Uist Division of the Hebridean Constabulary. I need a few minutes of your time.'

'That's a pity, darling, you see we're a bit busy right now,' said Dan Farquarson in an unmistakable Dundee accent.

This, Morag deduced from the quality of his clothes and Mollie's description had to be the business chappie with the big bankroll.

'Aye, maybe you could come back later, sweetheart,' added a big man sitting beside him with a pint of beer halfway to his mouth. He had the audacity to wink at her.

'I said my name is Sergeant Driscoll,' Morag reiterated assertively in her best no-nonsense voice. 'And this is official police business, so I am afraid that whether or not you are busy is of no consequence: I need to speak to you now.'

Bruce McNab had been sitting in shadows. He stood up swiftly and came forward, smiling placatingly. 'Morag Driscoll . . . I mean, Sergeant Driscoll, sorry. Of course you must ask whatever you want. Please, come in and sit down and let me introduce you to my clients.'

Morag let him make introductions while she swiftly appraised the group. The little middle-aged Dundee businessman was Dan Farquarson. His associate, whose size and bulging muscles made it obvious that he was in fact a minder, was Hugh Thompson — 'known to all as Wee Hughie', Dan Farquarson corrected with a laugh. Morag smiled at them mirthlessly, for chauvinism was a moral crime as far as she was concerned, and she was still rankling at the manner in which they had greeted her.

Then he introduced her to the last of the group, Sandy King, and her gaze lingered for what she realized may seem a moment overlong. The truth was that he ticked all of the right boxes as far as she was concerned. He was less than ten years younger than her, which wasn't an age apart, and with his long blond hair, square chin and china-blue eyes, she thought that he was quite the best-looking man she had seen in years. That and the fact that he was a football star whom she admired, brought a warmth to her cheeks.

'Can I order you a drink, Sergeant Driscoll?' he asked. Then, with a smile, 'Morag, you said your name was, didn't you?'

Morag shook her head and ignored his second question. 'This is official, I am afraid. I am here to ask you questions about a complaint that has been made against all of you.'

'A complaint!' exclaimed Wee Hughie, the minder. 'Who's looking for a kicking then?'

Morag turned steady eyes on him. 'We don't tolerate violence on West Uist, Mr Thompson.'

'Shush, Wee Hughie,' said Dan Farquarson, scowling at his associate. Then to Morag, 'What my friend meant to ask was what sort of complaint, Sergeant? And who made it?'

'Doctor Digby Dent, an entomologist working on the island, claims that one or more of you deliberately damaged a piece of his scientific equipment.' She produced a notebook and her silver pen. 'Now, if I can take a statement from each of you.'

'Ach, Morag Driscoll, is this really necessary?' voiced Bruce McNab. 'That Dent fellow is a nuisance. He puts everyone's back up.'

'A complaint has been made and I am duty bound to investigate it,' Morag replied, quite unperturbed. 'Now, you first, Mr McNab.'

Morag made neat entries as they each gave their account. She was not surprised to find that their versions were substantially the same as each other and that they were very different from Dr Dent's. Wee Hughie admitted that he had trodden on the pole, but had not realized that the net had been torn.

'It was an accident, Morag,' said Sandy King.

And on that point the others were quick to agree.

'You believe us, don't you, Morag?' Sandy King asked eagerly.

Morag felt the hairs on the back of her neck prickle, but she ignored them, just as she refused to be drawn into answering the question.

'I have noted all of your answers and I thank you. You have all been most helpful.'

'We would like to just draw a line under it,' said Dan Farquarson. 'It was an accident and no hard feelings to Dr Dent.'

Sandy King smiled at Morag. 'You can even say that I will be quite happy to reimburse the cost of his net, as a gesture of good will.' He held her regard for a moment then added, 'And maybe we'll see you again in a less official capacity?'

Morag lowered her eyes and felt her cheeks colour. 'Thank you, gentlemen,' she said.

'You all sound very reasonable.'

She snapped her notebook shut and was on the verge of asking Sandy King a casual question about the rumours over a transfer to the Picts, when she reconsidered and snapped back into professional mode.

'Just one final thing: Mollie said that you all came in dribs and drabs. Had you been apart since you left the river?'

Dan Farquarson was quick to answer. 'No, just visits to the toilet and that, you know. We've been together otherwise.' He looked over at Bruce McNab. 'That's right, isn't it, McNab?'

Bruce nodded with alacrity. 'Absolutely Mr Farquarson. Together all morning.'

IV

Torquil had taken Calum's call and agreed to pop round to the *Chronicle* offices. But first he took Crusoe for a walk along by the Mosset Burn that ran down from the moor behind the station to eventually run over a stretch of rapids before dropping into the sea.

Crusoe didn't seem to mind being put on a lead and walked alongside Torquil rather than straining at the lead.

'You've had a lead on before, haven't you,

Crusoe? And that means that you have had a proper owner.'

As if responding to the question Crusoe turned his head and barked once.

'Maybe I should just let you off the lead and see if you head off home.'

Crusoe turned his head again and barked twice.

Torquil laughed. 'Does that mean a 'no'? Well, my wee friend, I am planning to let you off the lead sometime. Maybe when I take you home to the manse. If no one claims you then you will have to get used to living with Uncle Lachlan and me for a while. And hopefully, with my girlfriend Lorna before too long.'

Suddenly Crusoe looked ahead and then stood stock still. Then he started to tremble. He barked and kept on barking, as if he was scared of something.

'What's the matter, boy?' Torquil asked. Then he looked ahead and realized. They were approaching the old humped-back bridge that spanned the Mosset Burn. Two young boys of about ten years of age, good lads whom Torquil recognized, were playing pooh sticks from the top of the bridge.

'Ah, I see. It brings back bad memories, does it, Crusoe? Of being tied to that timber and tossed in the water?'

Crusoe was showing whites of his eyes and his ears had gone back. He yelped and huddled in closer to Torquil.

'I want to get my hands on whoever did that to you,' Torquil said, crouching to give the dog a reassuring pat. 'If we only knew where they threw you in that might help.' He straightened and tugged gently on the lead. 'Come on, boy. It's time that I showed up at the *Chronicle* anyway. We'll nip through the back alley and do some investigating. If you are going to be a station dog, then I'll have to get you used to crime investigation.'

Three minutes later they were mounting the stairs of the *Chronicle* offices.

'Good grief! What's this, the new West Uist Police bloodhound?' Calum cried mischievously, as they appeared on the landing, where he and Cora were standing sipping mugs of tea.

Calum introduced Cora.

'And this is Crusoe,' said Torquil, bending to give the dog a pat. Immediately, Crusoe sat down, licked his hand and vigorously wagged his tail.

Torquil recounted the dog's history.

Calum frowned and Cora gave a gasp of horror. 'How could anyone be so cruel?' she said, squatting beside Crusoe and stroking his head. The collie responded with a whimper, then lay down and rolled over to accept further spoiling.

'Would you like me to put a piece in the *Chronicle*?' Calum asked. 'We could put up a reward for information.' He winked at Torquil. 'Or rather, the police could put up a reward of maybe twenty pounds?'

'Good idea, Calum my man. We can stretch to that if it helps us find who did this.'

Calum laid down his mug and rubbed his hands. 'Fine, consider it done. And, in fact, it will be Cora's first assignment as my cub reporter.'

Cora jumped to her feet and kissed Calum on the cheek, causing him to squirm with momentary embarrassment. Torquil saved him by pointing to the mess. 'So what happened here?'

He listened and jotted down the details. 'And you think that someone deliberately lured you out to Largo Head so that they could vandalize the office?'

'Pretty sure.'

'Any idea who?'

'No. As you know, a newspaperman makes the odd enemy along the way. It's an occupational hazard, as I was telling Miss Melville's great niece here.'

Torquil gaped. 'You are Miss Melville's great niece? Gosh, we had better mind our Ps and Qs or we'll have the old girl on our backs just like in the old days.'

Cora gave one of her effervescent laughs. 'Oh stop it! I don't believe my lovely old great aunt Bella would ever frighten anyone.'

Torquil and Calum stared at each other then laughed in unison.

'Not unless they were really naughty boys,' Cora added.

The *West Uist Chronicle* editor and the West Uist inspector of police both went silent and stared awkwardly at each other. Cora instantly picked up on the guilty look that passed between them.

'All right, Calum,' Torquil said. 'I'll get Ewan McPhee to come over in half an hour to photograph and dust the place.'

'Oh, I can do that afterwards,' Cora volunteered.

'I think he means he's going to dust the place for fingerprints, Cora,' Calum said with a grin.

'Oh!' exclaimed Cora. And it was her turn to blush.

V

It seemed as if half of the population of Kyleshiffin and a goodly number of tourists

90

and other folk from the outer parts of the island had squeezed into the Duncan Institute to watch the filming of the *Flotsam & Jetsam* show that evening.

The TV crew consisted of two cameramen, a soundman and the producer. Many of the audience, set-in-their-way islanders, had written them all off as a bunch of hippy-type, la-di-da luvvies with media studies degrees from a host of English universities. In this they were almost one hundred per cent wrong, since all of them were either Edinburgh or Dundee graduates in the arts or hard science. While Geordie Innes, the producer, looked like a fresh graduate, he was twenty-seven and had already won a coveted Dairsie Award for documentary making.

Lachlan and Kenneth were sitting in the front row, both wearing their dog collars. Lachlan had fleetingly seen Torquil before going in and been told about Crusoe, the prospective new resident of the St Ninian's manse. He was quite relaxed about it, although he had told Torquil that any house-training would be entirely his responsibility.

Morag was standing in the side aisle with her hands behind her back, while the Drummond twins were stationed at the back and other side of the hall, in the unlikely event of any trouble. She had seen Bruce McNab and his party of fishermen file into seats at the back of the hall. Chancing a glance over at them she saw Sandy King wink at her and she felt her heart skip a beat.

Don't be an idiot! she mentally chided herself. You're a police sergeant and you have three wee ones at home. Stop acting like a schoolgirl!

The stars of the show of course were Fergie Ferguson and his beautiful partner and co-presenter, Chrissie. Earlier in the after-noon they had met half of the audience at the pre-show antique viewing that they always did before an actual broadcast. Since they were planning ten twenty-minute programmes each evening Monday to Friday over the fortnight before the Scottish TV News bulletin they had been granted the use of the back room at the Duncan Institute every afternoon. People came with their antiques and knick-knacks and filed past Fergie and Chrissie as they sat at a central table. There they would give free valuations, occasionally make offers there and then, and essentially spot the antiques that they wanted people to return with to the show proper. They also primed them well, so that it would seem as if they were viewing the pieces for the first time on the show. It was a formula that had worked well for seven seasons and made the show something of a Scottish institution.

Fergie stood on the stage and gave the audience a final last-minute run through of the programme's format.

'So we would be grateful if everyone could just be careful of their language,' he said. 'No heckling, no lewdness, and, please, just remember that this is a family show.'

'There will be no swearing here, don't you worry, Mr Ferguson,' piped up Rab McNeish, the undertaker-carpenter, soberly dressed in his black funeral suit. 'There is no one who swears on West Uist.'

This was followed by general hilarity.

'Not from you in your burying suit, at any rate, Rab McNeish!' someone called out from the back of the hall, much to Rab's discomfiture. He moved restlessly in his seat and adjusted the old brown suitcase containing the treasures that he had already shown to Fergie at the pre-show viewing.

Fergie laughed good-naturedly and winked encouragingly at Rab. Then 'We'll be on the air in about five minutes. See you all then.'

He waved and went over to chat with Geordie Innes, the producer.

'Last call for snacks, folks,' called out Alec Anderson, as he stood at the left-hand steps leading up to the stage with his trolley of ice-cream, chocolates and crisps. 'Or if you would rather a cup of tea or coffee, my dear wife Agnes is at the back of the hall and will accommodate you.'

There was a last minute flurry of customers, then Travis, the soundman, gave them a two-minute bell. Finally, he addressed Fergie and Chrissie on the stage and counted them in before snapping the clapboard to start filming.

Fergie Ferguson gave a short show-biz laugh then immediately pitched in. 'Hello all you bargain hunters out there,' he said, flashing his Hollywood-white neatly capped teeth at the camera. 'Here we are again in Kyleshiffin, the main — no, the only town on West Uist for this edition of *Flotsam & Jetsam*!' He emphasized the name of the show and bent his knees to almost spring up with outstretched hands, like a latter-day circus master. And he held the smile and pose for a moment to allow Geordie Innes to merge the background picture of treasures washed up on a beach with the title of the show.

'And Kyleshiffin is going to be our home for the next fortnight. But before we look at some of the flotsam and jetsam that we have found on this island today, or which the good people of Kyleshiffin have brought along for us to value or bid for' — he waited for some canned laughter to come and go — 'we have been fortunate enough to have Dr Digby Dent, Scotland's most respected entomologist.' He put his hand to his mouth and gave a theatrical aside to the second camera. 'That means he studies insects, to you lot.'

He waited for a further burst of more canned laughter, which this time was accompanied by some genuine laughter from the audience. 'Dr Dent is kindly going to explain about the famous Scottish midges and why they have been such a scourge of the Scottish tourist industry over the years.' He turned his back to the audience and looked over his shoulder. 'Would you like me to show you what they did to me when I went for a swim?'

He squatted and thrust his bottom out and made as if to undo his trousers.

'Don't you dare, Fergie Ferguson,' quipped Chrissie with a mock scowl. 'It's bad enough that I had to put cream on those bites. Let's not inflict that on the good people here.'

Then Chrissie smiled and, with the cameras now on her, 'And so Dr Dent is also going to give us an insight into how the latest science is going to conquer the dreaded midge.'

There was an expectant hush, but Dr Dent

did not appear from the side door where Chrissie was pointing.

'We seem to have a technical hitch,' said Fergie, touching his ear, as if listening to a message relayed via an imaginary earphone. 'Bear with us, we shall — '

Dr Dent stumbled on to the stage from the other side, his inebriated demeanour apparent to all. Half of the audience gasped and half the audience giggled or chuckled with amusement.

'So you think we can get rid of the midges, do you?' he asked making his way directly for Chrissie, passing and ignoring Fergie who stood with an outstretched hand. 'There is little chance of that, I am afraid. *Culcoides impunctatus*, the highland midge has been around since the days of the dinosaur and they like this environment. It is the females that bite; they are always the more deadly of the species.' He leered at Chrissie and licked his lips. 'You know what I mean — Chrissie, isn't it?'

There was a ripple of scandalized outrage from the audience. Fergie Ferguson was generally used to dealing with awkward guests, but even he was taken slightly aback for a moment.

'Well thank you, Doctor Dent, I am sure that you want to get — '

Digby Dent turned and stared at him with bleary eyes. 'I don't want to get anything, my good man. I am here at your invitation to talk about the problem of the midge. You see, it is the female that bites, because she is a haematophagus insect. A blood-sucker, you see. And she needs to suck blood to develop her eggs.' He looked at Chrissie and smiled. 'She has sex first, then has to feed immediately after. What a life, eh?'

Chrissie tried to ignore him and stared into the camera. 'On the *Flotsam & Jetsam* show we do try to introduce some interesting guests. Tomorrow we hope to show an interview we are going to have with Guthrie Lovat, the famous West Uist beachcomber artist.'

This made Digby Dent prick up his ears. 'Lovat! I want to have a word with Lovat. Can I come along with you?' And he sidled uncomfortably close to Chrissie.

Fergie Ferguson started gesticulating to Geordie Innes the producer to cut the filming. Then he looked over at Morag and beckoned her on urgently.

Morag raised a hand to summon Douglas and Wallace Drummond and within seconds they had mounted the stairs and with an arm each, swiftly and silently frog-marched the protesting Dr Dent from the stage.

Fergie joined Chrissie whose cheeks had gone virtually crimson. 'Well, what do you know, eh, Chrissie? We've had all sorts of things brought to us before, but never anything quite so flotsam and jetsam as that piece of jetsam!'

'I think we should just jettison this part of the show, Fergie,' Chrissie said, recovering herself a little and turning towards him so that her considerable curves were in profile to the camera, a well-tried and tested ploy to divert a flagging audience. Geordie Innes meanwhile was frantically talking in his mobile phone to the mainland Scottish TV studio. He turned to Fergie and drew a hand across his throat to indicate immediate termination, then mouthed 'Twenty seconds.'

Fergie caught his gesture and nodded. 'Good idea, Chrissie,' he returned. And then, with an apologetic bow to the audience 'So sorry for this shemozzle folks. We're going to take a break from shooting for a few minutes and then hopefully we will be back on the air.'

Travis, the soundman, snapped the clapperboard and the TV crew immediately huddled together to consult, leaving the audience to erupt in shocked indignation.

'What the hell was that all about?' Fergie said, between gritted teeth to Morag who had entered the huddle. 'I want that bastard

98

charged. He's bloody well ruined our show on live TV. We'll be a laughing stock.'

Calum Steele was one of the few in the audience who had a smile on his face. Not only had he managed to take a couple of good pictures, but he had jotted down what had to be one of the best stories of the year.

VII

Dr Dent was held in the station cell for six hours after he was charged with being drunk and incapable, before Morag, as the duty officer, felt that he had sobered up enough to be released.

'Made an idiot of myself, eh?' was his parting question as Wallace and Douglas escorted him to the door. The twins grinned at Morag after seeing him off the premises.

'That's an understatement, isn't it, boys?' Morag said. 'Now come on, it is home time for us, too. I think we've had enough excitement for one day.'

As they set about closing down the station, Digby Dent set off with a slight stagger on the half-mile walk to his rented cottage. It was not long before he thought he heard footsteps behind him. He turned and squinted in the dark, but saw no one. He hurried on, crossed the beck and made his way up the dirt track at the end of which was the old stone cottage. He pushed open the wooden gate that opened on to the long gravel drive, at the end of which his old Land Rover was parked.

He had taken a couple of steps when he heard again the scrape of leather on gravel. He spun round and saw a figure several steps away. Then he recognized his pursuer.

'You!' His mouth curved into a sneer, then, 'What the hell do you want?'

He did not hear the second set of footsteps behind him. He felt an explosive pain over his right temple, then nothing.

4

Lachlan had slept fitfully, which was unusual for him. When dawn broke he rose, did his ablutions and dressed before going down-stairs to collect his clubs from their usual place in the hall. Alongside the wall a line of oil-stained newspapers protected the parquet floor from the assortment of carburettor components, oil filters and gears. They were all part of the ongoing project that he and Torquil were engaged in, to rebuild an Excelsior Talisman Twin Sports motor cycle.

His gaze hovered lovingly over these for a moment, and then he gave a start as he noticed something move in the shadows beyond the stripped-down carburettor.

'Goodness!' he exclaimed, after taking a sharp intake of breath. 'I forgot we had a new lodger.'

Crusoe looked out from the clothes basket that Torquil had placed at the far end of the hall and began furiously wagging his tail.

'At least you are not a noisy yapping wee chap,' Lachlan said, squatting and giving him a pat. 'That is a point in your favour right enough. Are you ready for a walk?'

Crusoe was instantly on his feet, his tail thrashing back and forth so much that it was literally wagging his body. Lachlan clipped the lead to his collar then slipped the loop over his wrist. Shouldering his golf bag he let himself out of the manse. Together they scrunched their way down the gravel path to the wrought-iron gate, then crossed the road to the stile that led directly on to the ten-acre plot of undulating dunes and machair that was St Ninian's golf course.

'We will walk over to the second hole then give you a wee test. If you can sit quietly each time I play a shot, then maybe I will be happy about you staying a bit longer with us at the manse.'

When they arrived at the tee Crusoe gave a soft bark and then as the Padre raised his finger to his lips and dropped the lead on the ground, he lay down and wagged his tail uncertainly.

Lachlan filled and lit his pipe. 'Good boy,' he nodded approvingly. 'It is looking as if you have had some training in dog manners,' he said with a grin. Then he pulled out his two wood and teed his ball up. 'Now for the acid test. Quiet on the tee while I drive off.'

After a couple of his usual waggles he

swung easily and the ball took off like a rocket and arced down the fairway into prime position for his second shot. The dog lay still and did not make a murmur.

'Hmm, maybe you've had a bit of gundog training. I certainly have never seen you on the course before so it is not a golfer that has trained you. You are a bit of a curiosity, Crusoe, my wee friend.' He picked up the bag and picked up the lead. 'We will play the second and the third, then we will go to the church where I will say my prayers.' He winked at the dog, who appeared to be listening to his every word as if understanding. 'That will include a prayer for you. Then we will play the eighth and ninth and get back in time to fix breakfast for Torquil.'

A couple of rabbits suddenly darted out of a cluster of gorse bushes and ran zig-zagging towards a nearby bunker. Crusoe barked three times and strained at the leash.

'Stay!' Lachlan snapped.

To his surprise, the dog instantly sat down.

'I am afraid that there would be no good chasing them, even if I let you off the lead. By the time you got to the bunker they would be down their burrows and I don't want to risk you getting stuck down one of them.'

Crusoe gave another bark, causing a flurry of movement over on the Padre's left. He grinned as half-a-dozen sheep broke into a run.

'And even though you are a collie, you will have to remember that dogs are not allowed to chase the sheep on the golf course.' He pointed the stem of his pipe at Crusoe. 'These sheep are precious, you see. They nibble the fairway grass down and make the course playable. They are our greenkeepers.'

Crusoe wagged his tail and looked after the retreating sheep but showed no sign of wanting to give chase. Lachlan scratched his chin. Crusoe was proving himself to be quite an enigma. Although he was still little more than a puppy, yet he had been trained to keep still and not to chase sheep. It was something he would tell Torquil about.

II

Torquil had slept like a log until his mobile phone roused him at seven. He answered it in a semi-doze, but when he heard his girlfriend, Lorna Golspie's voice he was instantly awake. Their conversation was typical of those still in the first flush of unbridled fresh love. At Lorna's news that she would be coming home for five whole days in a week's time his spirits had soared. Indeed, they soared so high that he rose, showered and prepared a breakfast of fried herrings in oatmeal before the Padre and Crusoe had returned.

'*Oh Mo chreach*! Oh dear me!' Lachlan exclaimed as they entered to the mouth-watering smell of the fish sizzling in the pan. 'Now this is a sight, Crusoe. My nephew is up and cooking breakfast with a smile on his face, and it is not even a pipe practice morning for him.'

Crusoe gave a small bark and a big wag of his tail.

'Lorna is coming home for five days next week,' Torquil volunteered. 'I don't know how she has wangled it with Superintendent Lumsden. I am so chuffed I am going to the cave to compose a piece to welcome her home.'

Lachlan washed his hands then sat down and unfurled his napkin. 'Ah, so it is an unscheduled pipe practice morning then! Will you be taking the dog? I have to say that I have been impressed with his patience so far. He sat and watched me play each shot and didn't want to chase the ball. He even wagged his tail when I hit a good shot.' He grinned. 'He was not quite so impressed with my putting though.'

Torquil laughed. 'Aye, it is curious that anyone could have been so cruel to him. I would like to get my hands on whoever cast him adrift like that.'

'Well, if it is any help, I would say that someone had started to train him as a gundog.' And he explained about the way that he lay down on the tee and about how he did not want to chase sheep. 'It sounds like he could belong to a farmer, or a crofter somewhere.'

Torquil frowned as he ladled fish on to his uncle's plate. 'I kept the cord that he was tied up with. I will be examining it later. There was something very curious about the knots. I didn't recognize them at all, and I have been messing about in boats all my life.'

Lachlan attacked his breakfast with gusto. 'And speaking of curious things, we came on one as we left the church. We went out through the cemetery to the eighth tee. There were fresh flowers on the grave of that lassie, Heather McQueen.'

Torquil stopped with his fork halfway to his mouth. 'The girl who drowned in Loch Hynish last year?' He suppressed a shiver at the thought. The loch was one of the island's beauty spots with its crannog and ruined castle in the middle, yet it held sad memories for him.[1]

---

[1] See *The Gathering Murders*.

'Aye. The curious thing is that whoever put those flowers there must have done so last evening or night. They definitely were not there when I showed Kenneth Canfield the grave yesterday.'

III

Ewan was due to take the catamaran *Seaspray* out for a round of the island's coastline later in the morning. Since that meant that he was more time-limited than usual, he decided to borrow Nippy, his mother's forty-year-old *Norman Nippy* 50cc moped, so that he could fit in a bit of hammer practice before he had to pick up the *Seaspray* from its harbour mooring. Borrowing Nippy was not something that he did lightly, for a 50cc moped was not the ideal vehicle for a self-conscious six foot four-inch hammer-throwing police constable. He was aware that he cut a slightly comedic figure and tried to ignore all of the winks, nudges and smirks as he went along.

Fortunately, there were not too many people on the road at seven in the morning, apart from the local shopkeepers and the market folk who were all up and about, setting up for the day's trade. He rode along

Habour Street nodding right and left to several of them.

Then the unexpected happened.

'Hey! Look out, you silly billy!' He cried as a canary yellow camper-van shot out of Weir Street and skidded for several feet as the driver slammed on his brakes. It stopped a yard over the halt line. Ewan had instinctively swerved and narrowly managed to swing round the front of the van just in time. He drew to a halt by the kerb, dismounted and switched off Nippy's engine. Hoisting the machine easily on to its stand he walked back as the driver slowly wound down his window.

'Ah! Sorry,' the man blustered. 'You are the — er — the hammer chappie, aren't you?'

Ewan eyed the two men appraisingly. Unlike the last time he had met them they were both smiling, albeit nervously. They both seemed embarrassed and concerned that they had almost knocked him off his moped.

'Aye, we are really sorry, Officer,' said the stocky, surly-looking one with the ear-ring who was sitting in the passenger's side. 'We are just anxious to get off to a place called the Wee Kingdom. We heard that there are sea otters off the coast there.'

'Eyes peeled!' Ewan said emphatically, causing both men to stare back at him in confusion. The truth was that he had verbalized the words that Torquil was forever telling him.

'Eyes peeled?' the driver repeated.

'Aye, you need to keep your eyes peeled,' Ewan told him firmly. 'That is what a good driver needs to remember. It doesn't matter if it is on one of those fancy motorways that they have on the mainland, or one of these back streets in Kyleshiffin. You have to be prepared for anything.' He gave them both one of his sternest looks. 'Please do not think of us as a bunch of yokels. We respect the law here on the island — and we impose it!'

The driver nodded. 'Understood, Officer. And we've learned our lesson. We'll have our eyes peeled from now on.'

Ewan gave them a final steely look then returned to Nippy to continue his journey up on to the moor.

Five minutes later he was doing his series of warm-up exercises. Then, after another five minutes he was whirling his hammer round and round before letting it fly up, out and away over the moor in a pleasingly long parabolic path to disappear in the heather. He grimaced at the splash of its landing, for there was always a chance of him losing it. But fortunately, its pole was sticking up in the air; a decided advantage that the Highland hammer had over the ball and wire design of the Olympic hammer.

He immediately started to pace out the distance, a grin spreading across his face as he did so, since it was a big throw.

'The porridge is working well today,' he mused to himself, as he reached the spot where his hammer was protruding from the other side of a tussock of gorse and heather. He reached over thigh high gorse and prepared to pull the hammer out of the bog. He grasped the handle and tugged so that it came away with a sucking, squelchy noise.

But, as it came out, so too did something else. A hazy cloud of midges suddenly rose from the bog and within moments Ewan was enveloped.

'Away with you all!' he cried, running backwards a few paces and almost tripping up. 'This new deodorant I have on is supposed to repel you little scunners.' He slapped himself where he felt bites and scratched his mane of hair. He turned and lifted his hammer so that he could beat a hastier retreat. Then he noticed that the ball was covered in a thick red fluid. He winced.

'Ugh! Blood?' he asked himself. 'Don't tell me I managed to land it in a dead sheep or something?'

Gingerly he crept back towards the tussock, waving his free hand for all he was worth to try to cut a swathe through the midge swarm. He peered over the gorse and then gasped in horror.

A man's body was lying face down in a bog pool, the brackish waters of which had been turned dark red by blood that had oozed out from a nasty head wound.

Ewan felt bile rise in his throat, for it was an ugly sight. He recognized the clothes only too well.

'My God! I killed him with my hammer!' he muttered, as he stared at the blood-soaked ball that dangled from its pole, then at the crushed head injury.

He stood for a moment in total shock, oblivious to the innumerable bites of the midge swarm.

IV

Cora had been almost dead on her feet by two o'clock in the morning when she and Calum had finally written up all of the articles and columns for the special issue of the *West Uist Chronicle*. Although it was officially a twice-weekly newspaper, whenever Calum felt that a special was needed, he duly produced it and the good folk of the island readily paid up and avidly read the extra gossip. Some weeks it was a daily event.

The main news that Calum wanted to impart related to the events surrounding the calamitous *Flotsam & Jetsam* TV show the previous evening. This in itself would not justify a whole paper, so he had shown Cora how to produce copy at the drop of a hat. To her delight he had allowed her to contribute, by writing up about the vandalism at the *Chronicle* office, as well as a short column about Crusoe the abandoned dog that Torquil McKinnon had found. He had been encouraging in his comments about her flowery style, which somewhat sweetened the bitter pill that she was forced to swallow as he slashed her 2,000 word article to a mere 1,000 with a few strokes of his blue editorial pencil.

'Brevity, lassie! That is the thing that you must concentrate on in a local paper. When you are the editor of a paper then you can let your literary juices flow freely. Until then, be concise, accurate and pithy. Like me!'

Cora had taken his words and his editing on the chin. She was determined to make a success of her journalism and was sure that her great-aunt Bella's advice to listen and learn from Calum Steele made great sense. She recalled the old lady telling her that although Calum Steele could be a puffed up little pipsqueak, yet he had a knack for telling the news. She remembered the exact expression she had used to describe his journalistic manner: 'He could speir the inside out of a clam!'

Cora had laughed at her great-aunt's use of the vernacular, for the word 'speir' actually meant to ask, to badger, rather than to use a weapon. Effectively, Calum could hector someone so mercilessly that they would give him a story as if their life depended upon it.

When Calum had insisted that she go home at two o'clock she had gone with some reluctance, promising to return by seven at the start of the new day. Calum had bartered for eight, which he thought would give him an extra hour to recover from the very large whisky that he had mentally promised himself once he had completed and printed the special issue, then mobilized his paper boys.

As it happened, it was three large whiskies, so he was in a deep sleep when Cora mounted the stairs in a state of great excitement at eight in the morning with a copy of the *Chronicle* bought from Staig's.

'My first ever proper published story!' she cried, mounting the stairs three at a time. 'Oh thank you, Calum! Thank you!'

'Wh-What!' Calum stammered, blinking and fumbling to find his wire-framed spectacles which had fallen astray when he had slumped back on his camp-bed. He held up his hands to stop her further advance, as if she was a bounding puppy about to hurtle herself at him. 'Look, Cora lassie, you are making a habit of this.'

Cora giggled. 'Of what? Seeing you in bed?'

Calum squirmed with embarrassment. 'Ah — er — don't be cheeky, lassie. I'll have you know that I — '

'I was just kidding, Calum.' She replied. 'Don't worry, I won't tell Great-aunt Bella.'

'Tell what to Miss Melville?' he asked quickly, his eyes wide open in alarm behind his spectacles.

'That you like to drink whisky so early in the morning.'

Calum looked at her in shock. 'What are you talking about, lassie? I never drink too early. I drink a bit late sometimes. What is late to a journalist may seem early to someone else.' He wagged his finger in admonishment. 'If you want to be a good journalist, you have a lot to learn. I insist on accuracy from my staff, Cora.'

He stood up and hiccupped. 'So, how about a cup of tea and then I will treat you to a really good greasy breakfast at the Friar Tuck Café?'

Cora grimaced. 'That's kind of you,

Calum, but I am a bit of a vegetarian, actually. And I never eat anything greasy, not even chips.' Then she gave him one of her sudden smiles. 'But I'll put the kettle on for a cup of tea.'

And before he could take in what he considered her admission of food heresy, she disappeared into the kitchenette.

'That was a great article you wrote, boss,' she called out. 'That Dr Digby Dent will have a horrible headache when he wakes up. I expect he will feel such a fool.'

'Aye, it is always best to avoid a hangover,' Calum replied with a yawn, as he massaged his own aching temples.

His mobile phone went off and he answered it automatically.

When Cora came in a few moments later with a couple of mugs of steaming tea she found him listening to a voice on the other end, his jaw hanging open and his eyes staring into space.

'Up on the moor, you say? Aye, I will go straight away. And so who are — ?'

He frowned then looked in consternation at the phone.

'Tea!' Cora said, handing the mug to him.

He shook his head and reached for his yellow anorak. 'No time, Cora. Grab those helmets, we have work to do. You were almost right about Dr Dent and his head. He would have a headache — if he was still alive to feel it. He's been found up on the moor with his head bashed in.'

Cora's face went ashen and she dropped the mug of tea at his feet.

He was about to mumble something about his good carpet when she pitched forward in a dead faint on to his camp-bed.

V

The chain of communication had clicked into action straight away. Ewan had called Morag on his mobile, then she had contacted Torquil and set the ball rolling.

Torquil had been the first on the scene, zooming up the hill from Harbour Street on his Bullet, with Crusoe peering out of one pannier and his pipes from the other. He had been intending to go to St Ninian's Cave to try out a new piece that he had been working out in his head ever since Lorna had rung that morning.

He was only a few moments ahead of Dr Ralph McLelland in the Kyleshiffin ambulance. It was not a purpose-built vehicle, but an ancient converted camper-van which had been donated by a former laird of Kyleshiffin.

They had both been briefed by a pasty-faced Ewan McPhee, who looked wretched and cold, with vomit stains down his T-shirt and numerous blotches about his head and neck.

'I didn't mean to do it, Torquil!' Ewan said. 'How was I to know that he was lying there in the heather? I . . . I . . . '

Torquil patted his shoulder. 'Of course you didn't know that, Ewan. Now just calm down. Here,' he said, handing him Crusoe's lead, 'you look after the dog while we have a proper look.'

Crusoe was snapping right and left at invisible midges.

'Aye, the midges are bad this morning,' Ewan said, as he took the lead and led them over towards the tussock of heather and gorse where the body lay.

He explained that upon recovering from his initial shock he had hauled it out of the bog to see if he could try resuscitation, but it had been all too clear that the man had been beyond such help. Even so, he had placed him in the recovery position.

'Strange that the midges don't seem to land on him,' Ewan remarked. 'They just home in on us.'

Dr McLelland knelt beside the body, ignoring the fact that brackish peat water had soaked into his corduroy trousers. 'It is because they only feed off the living. They are attracted to the carbon dioxide that animals breathe out.'

'I didn't know that, Doctor McLelland,' Ewan said.

'Nor did I until the other day; Doctor Dent here told me himself.'

Torquil said nothing, but watched as the doctor opened his bag and pulled out his stethoscope and an ophthalmoscope. He knew from experience that he would perform his examination strictly to the letter, leaving nothing to chance and risking no error in his analysis.

The doctor was one of Torquil's oldest friends. Along with Calum Steele, the three of them had thought themselves to be like the Three Musketeers when they were attending the Kyleshiffin School under Miss Bella Melville's watchful eye. Then they had grown up and gone their separate ways: Torquil to study law and become a police officer; Calum to throw himself into journalism; Ralph to study medicine. After graduating from Glasgow University Ralph had fully intended becoming a pathologist and had studied forensic medicine and medical jurisprudence, until his uncle had suddenly died. Family loyalty had then overcome personal academic ambition and he returned to West Uist to take over the old boy's medical practice, as well as his post as honorary police surgeon to the West Uist Division of the Hebridean Constabulary. On several occasions in the past his forensic skills had come in very handy.

'So can you give an estimate on how long he has been dead?' Torquil asked, as he looked over Ralph's shoulder.

'Hard to be precise,' he replied pensively. 'What with the chance of accelerated rigor mortis if he had been in this cold peat water for any time, it could be as little as two hours or as long as twenty-four.'

'You . . . you mean that I didn't kill him with the hammer?' Ewan blurted out.

'No, you definitely did not. He has been dead for a good while,' Ralph replied. 'I don't think that your hammer even touched him. It just happened to land in the bog beside him. It looks as if he fell and bashed his head on this jagged rock here.' He pointed to a blood-soaked rock that was protruding from the pool. 'As I say, he could have been here for a whole day.'

'Except that he was in police custody last night,' Torquil said. 'You must have heard about the rumpus he created on the *Flotsam & Jetsam* TV show that they were filming?'

Ralph looked round and shook his head. 'I

was out on an emergency case all evening. The devil's own job I had in stabilizing the patient.'

'Well, we didn't release him until ten-thirty,' Ewan volunteered. 'Morag reckoned he had sobered up enough by then.'

Ralph bent over the dead man's lips and sniffed. He clicked his tongue. 'I'll need to check his alcohol level when I do the post-mortem. Assuming you want a post-mortem, Torquil?'

'Are you able to say how he died?' Torquil asked. 'Not meaning to be facetious, Ralph.'

'I would guess that he'd gone for a walk up here on the moor, still inebriated, and tipped and bashed his head. Could have been the head injury that killed him, or he could have drowned in the bog.' He pushed himself to his feet and gave a thin, humourless smile. 'But that is not my brief, is it? It is only my initial opinion. I would need to do a post-mortem to determine the cause of his death.'

They all turned at the sound of a click. Calum Steele and Cora Melville were standing a few paces behind them. Calum had a digital camera in one hand and his customary spiral notebook in the other. He was gripping his pen between his teeth.

'Calum! What do you mean by sneaking up

on us like that?' Torquil snapped. He knew only too well that his friend was full of journalistic guile having fancied himself as an investigative reporter since his schooldays. Despite his portly frame, when he sensed that a story demanded it, he could move with the stealth of a cat. And when he was in his investigative journalist mode, loyalty and friendship came second best to the prospect of a scoop.

'Just answering a tip-off, Inspector McKinnon,' Calum replied, immediately moving to a professional footing. 'So, as I understand it, you have found Dr Digby Dent dead on the moor, seemingly having fallen and bashed his head, although there is a question as to whether he had been bludgeoned with a Highland hammer.'

Ralph scowled at Calum. 'If you have been eavesdropping for long, Calum Steele, then you will have heard me say he was not hit by Ewan's hammer.'

Calum shrugged as he handed the camera to his pale-faced assistant. He jotted a couple of words in his notebook. 'OK, so then he may or may not have drowned after falling and bumping his head, but as I see it there is a crucial question that has yet to be answered.'

Torquil eyed his friend suspiciously. 'And

what question is that, Mr Steele?'

'Upon what basis did the West Uist Police deem that it was safe to release him from custody? You see, from where I am standing it seems certain that if he had been kept in custody he would still be alive right now.' He drew a line under his last note. 'Some folk might use the N word for that. Negligence, I mean.'

He looked his best friend straight in the eye.

'Would you care to make a statement to the Press, Inspector McKinnon?'

VI

Wallace and Douglas had been out in their old fishing boat, earning their living by catching herrings, just as their father and his father had done before them. They were returning with a good catch and appropriately high spirits.

'Look to starboard,' Wallace called above the engine noise. 'It looks like old Guthrie Lovat is out in his *Sea Beastie*.'

'Aye! We haven't seen him about these waters for a while.'

Wallace gave a blast on the boat's horn and they both waved.

The *Sea Beastie* had at one time been a common sight about the island until Guthrie had become famous. At least, that was how many of the locals described his change to become a recluse.

Guthrie Lovat stepped out of his cabin, his luxuriant beard catching the wind. He screwed up his eyes and, with a hand over them to shield them from the sun, he peered back at the Drummond twins. Then, recognizing them he waved back.

'How is the beachombing going?' Wallace called across.

'Pretty fair,' Guthrie called back. 'But it could be better!' He lifted his left arm and gestured to his wrist, as if pointing at his watch. 'Can't stop though. I need to get out to the Cruadalach Isles.' He waved again then went back into his cabin. There was a roar and the *Sea Beastie* accelerated away.

The twins waved after him.

'A man of few words, eh?' Wallace remarked.

'Aye, a surly bugger and no mistaking. Maybe he's on a par with that Dr Dent fellow.' Douglas grinned.

The brothers laughed, for they had found the whole *Flotsam & Jetsam* débâcle utterly hilarious.

Wallace adjusted their course and they

headed in the direction of Kylshiffin harbour.

'It is a funny thing, Wallace, but shouldn't our esteemed PC Ewan McPhee be out and about in the *Seaspray* by now?' Douglas remarked.

Wallace guffawed. 'Aye, he should. But the big galoot might have slept in again.'

'Or maybe he lost his hammer up on the moor again?'

'I can just imagine him up there now, getting bitten to death by the midges.'

At this they dissolved into another fit of mirth.

VII

Cora was not sure how she felt. She had never seen a dead body before and although she had not fainted up on the moor she had found the whole encounter most embarrassing. They had returned to the *Chronicle* offices where Calum had immediately set about preparing for yet another special edition.

'This is what you wanted, isn't it, Cora?' he asked, as he tapped away on his laptop. 'Real cutting-edge journalism. And what a follow up to last night's story. The readers will love this.'

'But aren't you worried about upsetting Inspector McKinnon and the others?'

'I am a responsible journalist, Cora. I am not in this for popularity. It is my responsibility to present the facts to the reading public.'

'But are you serious about saying there was police negligence?'

Calum heaved a sigh and swivelled round in his chair. 'There is nothing personal in this, Cora. Torquil will understand that.'

'But he looked sort of — well — uncomfortable.' She wrinkled her nose. 'As if you were betraying him, sort of.'

'Havers, lassie!'

'And PC McPhee looked so upset.'

'A man in police custody was set free and is found dead hours later, Cora. If they had kept him he would be alive now.' He pushed his wire-frame spectacles further back on his nose. 'Look, I want you to help. While I am writing this up and setting up the issue I want you to go and interview Sergeant Driscoll at the station. She was the duty sergeant last night. While you are there, you can also make enquiries about what progress they have made about the break-in at the offices here.'

'Do I have to?' Cora pleaded. 'Surely they won't have any news.'

'Of course they won't. But that's not the point, is it?'

'And the point is?'

'To keep them on their toes and show them that the *Chronicle* means business. Now off you go, I have a phone call that I need to make.' He winked at her as he reached for his mobile. 'It will do no harm to let Scottish TV know that we're on to a big story.'

VIII

The yellow camper-van turned off the coastal road and took the dirt track up to the row of derelict, crofters' cottages. It swung round behind them so that it was unseen from the road.

'Come on, Craig,' said the driver, the leaner of the two. 'The sooner we get the stuff stashed the better.'

Once outside Craig cursed. 'Huh! I'm not so keen on this place, Tosh. It's us that takes all the risks.'

'Don't start that again. We do what the boss tells us to do.'

'The boss! I'm getting fed up with him too.'

The crunch of a foot on gravel made them both spin round, their eyes open in alarm. Craig's hand darted inside his jacket to the heavy object that he kept hidden there.

'So you are getting fed up with me, are

126

you?' a voice snapped.

'Craig was just joking, boss,' Tosh replied with an uncertain grin.

'As if I give a toss! Just tell me. Did you do it, and did you make sure no one saw you?'

Craig and Tosh glanced nervously at each other then the one called Tosh nodded. 'Aye, we did it all right.'

Neither of them fancied telling their boss about their encounter with PC McPhee.

5

I

Morag stared at Cora in dumbfounded amazement.

'And Calum Steele told you to ask me that? Just how long have you been his assistant?'

Cora squirmed. 'Er — since yesterday, Sergeant Driscoll.'

'Since yesterday?'

Cora felt flustered and nodded apologetically.

'Then I suggest that you should tell the editor of the *West Uist Chronicle* to do his own dirty work. If he wants a statement from the West Uist Division of the Hebridean Constabulary, he should go about it through the proper channels, instead of sending his new assistant.'

Cora bit her lip. 'And — er — what are the proper channels, Sergeant?'

Morag smiled humourlessly. 'He should make a formal request in person to the officer on duty — me!'

Cora was already backing towards the

door. 'I will tell him that, Sergeant Driscoll.'

She was about to reach for the door when she remembered the other task that he had given her. 'Oops! Sorry! There was something else I need to ask you.'

'Ask away then.'

'Have you — er — any news on your investigation into the break-in at the *Chronicle* offices?'

Two pinpricks of colour appeared on Morag's cheeks and started to expand as her eyes grew wider.

Cora instinctively tensed her neck muscles, expecting a torrent of ire. But inexplicably, Morag's expression suddenly softened and she smiled.

'Nothing yet, Miss Melville, but I will be happy to update Mr Steele when he comes to see me.'

'Ah . . . thanks, I . . . ' Cora began. But the door suddenly shot open and knocked her in the back, propelling her forward.

'Oh good grief!' called Wallace Drummond, entering and shooting a hand out to catch the stumbling Cora before she pitched on to her face. 'So sorry, miss. I was in such a hurry. I haven't hurt you, I hope?'

Cora recovered her balance and turned to find herself looking up at the smiling face of Wallace Drummond, with an identical face appearing a second later to grin over his shoulder.

'You will have to excuse my brother. He is a bit heavy-handed,' explained Douglas, sweeping off his fisherman's bobble hat at the same time as he plucked off his twin's. 'Whoever would think that two gowks like us could be special police constables!'

Morag slapped the counter to gain attention and the trio looked round at her.

'If you two would let go of Miss Melville's great-niece, then she will be able to get back to her new job as Calum Steele's cub reporter.'

Cora blushed then nodded at them before hastily dodging between them to let herself out.

Wallace stood looking bemused. 'Sorry, Morag, did we miss something there? It seemed that you and that lassie were having some sort of a tiff. And did you say that she was Miss Melville's something-or-other?'

Morag raised the counter-flap and beckoned them through. 'Three rights! Yes, you did miss something. Yes, I am in a mood with her. And yes, she is Miss Melville's great-niece.'

Douglas gave a short laugh. 'Well whoever would have thought that the old girl could have such a beautiful looking relative! Cora, did you say her name was?'

Morag scowled at him. 'It is not funny, Douglas. She is working for the *Chronicle* and Calum sent her over to ask about why I released Dr Dent last night.'

Then to the twins' surprise she slumped forward, slapping her elbows on the counter and burying her face in her hands. 'Oh God!' she cried.

The twins reacted in unison as they often did. They both put an arm about her shoulders.

'What is wrong, Morag Driscoll?'

'Aye, tell us.'

Morag sighed and shoved herself to her feet. She patted both their hands. 'It looks as if it was a bad mistake. Ewan found him this morning up on the moor, lying in a bog pool with blood everywhere. When he phoned in he thought he must have bashed his brains out with his hammer.'

Both Wallace and Douglas stared back at her, their faces draining of colour.

'Torquil phoned me a bit later,' she went on. 'Ralph McLelland had examined the body. He was pretty sure that he was dead already, and he had doubts about whether the hammer had actually touched him. It might just have landed in the pool near him.'

Douglas let out a soft whistle. 'Thank goodness for that.'

'But what is Calum Steele on about?' Wallace asked.

'He is implying police negligence. If I had kept him in custody last night he would still be alive.'

Wallace punched one hand against the other. 'Let me go round and see the wee scunner, Sergeant. I'll point out the error of his ways.'

Morag gave him a wan smile. 'I don't think that would help very much at the moment, my wee darling.'

'No, but it might make us feel better,' said Douglas, through gritted teeth.

II

The Reverend Kenneth Canfield woke to find himself in a world of pain. His head felt as if it was about to explode, his eyes felt as if they had been sand-blasted, and as he opened them the morning sun seemed to sear them causing him to shut them tightly again. Then a wave of nausea hit him like a battering ram and he struggled to roll over so that he could vomit on the floor and not in his bed.

His stomach jettisoned its contents and he lay retching for several minutes before he felt able to lie back and piece together his fragmented memories of the night before. He began by slowly prising his eyes open to confirm that he was back in his room at the Commercial Hotel.

'Oh Lord, what have I done?' he groaned. 'The whisky will be the death of me one of these days.'

The image of him having a large whisky with Lachlan McKinnon flooded back.

'Ah, that was the first of them, you fool. You should have stuck to drinking tea. Now Lachlan may suspect my weakness.'

Then he saw himself striding towards Dr Digby Dent's cottage later on — being admitted — offered whisky — then arguing.

'Oh man! I should not have drunk whisky with him. What was I thinking of when I went there to confront him?'

Then the memory became more blurred. There was more whisky — good whisky, he remembered — the two of them arguing and then coming to some agreement, before arguing again. And finally, just a blur until he made it back to the Commercial Hotel.

'My word! The hotel folk will have seen me as drunk as a skunk. Me! A man of the cloth who should know better, who should behave himself.'

There was a knock on the door then a concerned voice.

'Are you all right in there, Minister? I

thought I heard you being sick. Are you needing a doctor?'

'No doctor, thank you,' he called out, trying to sound as normal as possible. 'I think I may have a bit of a tummy bug. I will be OK.'

With some relief he heard footsteps receding down the corridor.

But would he be OK? It would help, he thought, if he could just remember what had happened.

The worrying thing was all the guilt that he felt. He had a nagging fear that it was not just because he had got drunk with Dr Dent.

III

Bruce McNab was in an ill humour as he paced back and forth by the berth of *The Mermaid*, his thirty-foot fishing cruiser. As far as he recalled, the arrangements for the day had been firmly agreed. He had given his party the choice of sea-fishing in the waters out towards Iona, or snipe shooting up on the Hoolish Moor. The discussion about which they should do had been interesting and amusing, for a short time. Then it had turned into a right old drinking session.

'Damn the whisky!' he grumbled to himself as he felt a fresh stab of pain in his head. 'It clouds the brain, makes folk argue and — forget everything!'

He massaged his now throbbing temples, which reminded him that he had gone well past his usual limit during the session. All of them seemed to have, except, he dimly recollected, Sandy King. The professional footballer had taken just a couple of drams then gone on to shandies.

'Sensible lad!' Bruce remarked to himself. Then he frowned with irritation. 'But if he didn't drink, why is he not here?'

It had all started after they watched that Dent idiot making a fool of himself on TV. Dan Farquarson had ordered a round of Glen Corlans to celebrate. Then Bruce had reciprocated, followed by Wee Hughie. Soon after that his memory of the night failed.

Doubt then started to creep into his mind. Was he the one who had got it wrong? Were they waiting for him up on the moor?

'Pah! Why don't any of them answer their mobiles? Damn it!'

After another ten minutes he concluded that they were definitely not coming, so he stowed the sea-rods back in their cupboard and locked up *The Mermaid* before heading back home.

'Why worry, Bruce, you fool,' he told himself. 'They have paid already, so it is no skin off my nose if they have missed their sport.'

He climbed into his old jeep and drove towards home.

His two chocolate Labrador gundogs were barking their heads off as he came up the drive.

What is up with them? he mused as he drew up before his log-cabin. It is not like them to be going daft like this.

Then he saw the cabin door standing ajar.

'Bloody hell! It has been forced!' He cursed as he picked up a piece of timber and stealthily approached, grateful that the dogs did not stop their barking in case that could alert anyone still inside.

There was no one there, but the inside looked as if a tornado had wrecked the place.

Bruce McNab had the trained eye of a hunter. He recognized false trails when he saw them. The chaos around him was contrived, he had no doubt.

Whoever had broken into his cabin and thrown things hither and thither had done so with a definite purpose in mind.

He felt his heart speed up, since he had a pretty good idea what they were looking for.

IV

Fergie and Chrissie had started the day as they usually did, with passionate love-making.

136

Like so many people in show-biz they often found it hard to come back to bland real life after the buzz of performing. Yet, while so many celebrities turned to drugs or alcohol, they turned to sex. Lots of it. It suited them perfectly, for they were both blessed with a high libido. All of their TV crew knew and accepted this as the norm and treated their impromptu absences for the odd hour as a bit of a joke. 'Bonk breaks,' they called them, behind their backs. Yet the thing that everyone found most curious was the fact that they never directed their libidos at anyone else. All of their flirting was just an act; for the truth was they were still just as deeply in love as when they had first met.

'I love looking at you first thing in the morning,' Fergie cooed, as he lay stroking Chrissie's hair.

'And I do, too,' Chrissie replied with a mischievous smile as she leaned towards him to plant a kiss on the smooth dome of his forehead, which was only ever seen by her, it usually being covered by the hairpiece that lay on the bedside cabinet.

'It's going to be an exciting day, Chrissie. I can feel it in my bones. Getting Guthrie Lovat on the show should make up for the fiasco we had with Digby Dent last night.'

Chrissie giggled. 'But it was so funny when

you think about it, lover. I mean, he made an idiot of himself and folk would have laughed, but all publicity is good. All of Scotland will be talking about it this morning.'

There was a rustle outside the door then the rattle of a tray of crockery being laid on the floor. A tap on the door was followed by a cough then the announcementf, 'Your breakfast and paper, Mr Ferguson.'

Chrissie popped out of bed and pulled on a flimsy dressing-gown before unlocking the door to bring in the tray.

Fergie took the *Chronicle* from the tray and smoothed it out on his knees. A large photograph of a drunken Dr Digby Dent lurching towards a startled Chrissie while Fergie looked on in shocked horror, was emblazoned with the headline:

FLOTSAM & DRUNKSUM!
THE MIDGE MAN GETS A FLEA IN HIS EAR!

Fergie laughed. 'You are right as ever, Chrissie. Even bad publicity should help the ratings. Everyone is bound to watch tonight.' He scanned the article then shook his head. 'What an idiot that Dent lad is. And I thought he was a respectable scientist.'

'Even scientists can be drunks, darling. Come on now, let's have breakfast, then we — '

The sound of footsteps coming along the corridor was followed by a staccato rapping on the door.

'Fergie! It's me, Geordie! Let me in will you?'

'Geordie? We're having breakfast,' Fergie called back irritably.

'It's urgent. Let me in!'

Fergie snatched up his hairpiece and deftly put it on. Once Chrissie gave him a nod of approval he climbed out of bed, dragging a sheet with him to wrap toga-style about him. He strode across the room and imperiously pulled the door open, as if he actually was an emperor of Rome.

Geordie Innes slid past him, his face the epitome of bad news. 'I just had a phone call from Guthrie Lovat. He's changed his mind. He won't come on the show tonight.'

'Wh . . . Wh . . . Why not?' Fergie spluttered.

'It was a done deal,' Chrissie added.

Geordie Innes glanced over at Chrissie, sitting by the dressing-table, her dressing-gown doing little to conceal her feminine charms. He unconsciously licked his lips before turning back to Fergie.

'He saw the show last night, didn't he? He said he hadn't realized the sort of programme it was.' Geordie swallowed hard, his Adam's apple bobbing up and down nervously. 'He said we could stick our show!'

Fergie's cheeks reddened.

Then Chrissie voiced the thought that had been bubbling up in her mind.

'Look's like we were wrong, Fergie, my love. Sometimes bad publicity is just bad publicity.'

V

Torquil was sitting behind his desk stroking Crusoe as he listened to Morag's account of Cora Melville's visit. The Drummond twins stood leaning on either side of a filing cabinet, while Ewan was standing by the door so that he could hear if anyone came into the station.

'I could cheerfully throttle Calum Steele sometimes,' she said. 'Fancy him sending that young girl to do his dirty work.'

'Aye, but we shouldn't shoot the messenger,' said Wallace.

'Especially not such a bonnie one, at any rate,' agreed his brother.

Ewan clicked his tongue disapprovingly. 'You two need to take things a bit more seriously.'

'I am serious,' Douglas protested. 'She is really bonnie.'

Torquil gave Crusoe a final pat then drew his chair up to the desk. 'Ewan is right, lads. There is a serious issue here. A man that we had taken into custody has been found dead just a few hours after we released him.'

'After I released him,' Morag corrected. 'It is my responsibility.'

'Ours too,' Wallace promptly put in. 'We saw him and we agreed with you. He was sober enough to get home on his own.'

'Absolutely,' Douglas agreed. 'Solidarity, that is what we have in West Uist. All for one and one for all, and all that.'

Morag gave them a weary smile. 'I appreciate that, boys, but, as I said, it was my responsibility. I made the decision.'

Torquil shook his head. 'As a matter of fact, Morag, as the officer in charge, the responsibility is all mine. Yet before we all start self-flagellating, let us be clear about the whole thing: was it your honest opinion that it was safe to let Dr Dent go home?'

'With my hand on my heart, Torquil, I thought he was sober enough, yes.'

'And you lads?'

The Drummonds looked at each other and curtly nodded. 'Us too,' Wallace declared for them.

'In that case I would be quite happy to make a statement backing my officers.'

Morag's jaw dropped. 'You mean that you are going to talk to that wee gutter-snipe, Calum Steele?'

Torquil grinned. 'I didn't say that. I said

that I would be happy to make a statement, but only to a responsible journalist. Calum Steel no longer fits that bill and from now on is *persona non grata* in this station.'

Ewan's face lit up. 'Is that official, boss? Can I show him the door if he sneaks in?'

'If I am here I will talk to him, or rather, I'll give him a talking to. If I'm not in, then it is official and he can be shown the door.'

Then he turned to the twins. 'And the same thing goes for any other representatives of the *West Uist Chronicle*. If in doubt, refer them to me. Do you understand, lads?'

Wallace and Douglas looked crestfallen.

'It's understood, Torquil,' said Wallace.

Douglas sighed and flicked his eyes ceilingwards. 'Aye, like I said, solidarity.'

VI

Calum was in his element. He had rung Scottish TV and eventually managed to get through to Kirstie Macroon. He had given her the outline story about Dr Digby Dent's death and the finding of the body on the moor by the hammer-throwing PC Ewan McPhee. As he expected she just about bit his hand off for the story and so set up an impromptu telephone interview with him. It was something

142

that he had done several times in the past. When the News programme went out they would show the stock photograph that they held of Calum, showing him posing in front of his Remington typewriter wearing a bow tie, braces and with his hair slicked down. Then they would play the interview with a little crackling in the background to illustrate both the remoteness of the affair and Scottish TV's vigilance and diligence in bringing the news from places as remote as West Uist.

Calum found that these exposures always boosted sales of the *Chronicle*, both on West Uist and on the other islands the day after.

He was still glowing with pleasure at the thought of his scoop, but even more so at having actually been talking to Kirstie Macroon, when Cora slowly mounted the stairs and slumped down on the settee.

'That was awful, Calum,' she groaned. 'I hated that job.'

'Did she give you a good statement?' Calum asked with a grin.

'She gave me a flea in my ear, more like. I have never been so embarrassed in my life.'

'Well, you'll need to toughen up, Cora. A journalist has to have a tough hide.'

'Don't you ever — well — er — feel disloyal to your friends?'

Calum pursed his lips for a moment. Then

he shrugged and began typing a few notes on his laptop.

'Never thought about it, lassie. My job is to tell the news, not make friends. Oh, and to sell newspapers, of course!'

Cora stared at him in disbelief for a moment. But it was only for a moment. She began to wonder.

VII

Rab McNeish had been busy preparing a body all night.

It had been an unusual undertaking, as the deceased had lived on the island of Benbecula all of his life, only announcing on his death bed that he wanted to be buried on his native West Uist. Accordingly, after all the red tape had been dealt with Rab had gone out on the evening ferry and returned on the special fuel ferry with the body in a temporary coffin in the back of his carpenter's van.

He had gone straight to his chapel of rest and set about preparing the body in the embalming-room in readiness for the relatives to view him at noon.

'And tired out, is what I am,' he sighed, as he left the chapel and made his way back to his home, a sprawling croft with outhouses and work sheds on Sharkey's Boot, the curiously shaped peninsula beyond the star-shaped Wee Kingdom on the west of the island.

'A wee sleep and a bath to revive me and then I'll be presentable for the relatives at noon.'

But as he drove along the leg of the Boot towards his croft he suddenly felt his heart skip a beat.

The front door was standing open and a panel had been kicked in. 'My Lord!' he breathed, braking hard.

He reached over the passenger's seat and grasped a claw hammer.

'Please Lord don't let anyone have found me out!'

VIII

Wee Hughie had never known when to stop once he got going. The night before had been such a time, the result being that he had so much alcohol in him that if he had been left to his own devices, he would have slept around the clock.

'Get up, Wee Hughie,' Dan Farquarson said sharply, as he shook him awake. 'It's after eleven and we should have gone shooting or fishing with McNab and Sandy.'

Wee Hughie clutched his head and blinked

his way back to painful consciousness. 'Crivens! We must have had a skinful last night, boss. Look at me; I didn't even manage to get undressed.'

'Me neither,' replied a crumpled looking Dan Farquarson. 'And the Lord only knows where Sandy is. It looks as if he's gone off without us.'

'Gone shooting?'

Despite himself, Dan Farquarson laughed. 'Sandy King has gone shooting! That's a good one, Wee Hughie. Very droll.'

Wee Hughie rose to his feet, pleased to think that his boss had thought he had deliberately made a joke.

Dan Farquarson shook his head. 'But this is all going wrong. I rented this luxury cottage here in the back of beyond and booked this hunting and shooting trip with the Hebrides' very own Crocodile Dundee so that we could get Sandy away from the limelight long enough for us to have a good meeting.' He slumped down on the edge of Wee Hughie's newly vacated bed and thumped the bedside table. 'But nothing is going to plan.'

Neither of them heard the footsteps in the hall.

'And just what plans would those be, Mr Farquarson?' asked Sandy King. He stood in the doorway, dressed in a black track suit and trainers. 'I think it is time that we put our cards on the table, don't you?'

IX

Early that evening Calum and Cora stationed themselves at a table in the lounge bar of the Bonnie Prince Charlie right in front of the big plasma TV screen. As news of Dr Digby Dent's sudden death had already travelled round the island by old-fashioned bush telegraph the bar was full, as people had flocked in to have a drink while they listened to the news. Mollie McFadden and her staff were doing a roaring trade.

The background chatter suddenly stopped when the Scottish TV news signature tune came on.

'She's pretty, isn't she?' Cora whispered to Calum, when Kirstie Macroon appeared.

Calum grunted and beetled his brows to indicate that he wanted to listen. Cora sat back, suitably rebuked.

And then Kirstie Macroon was reading out the headlines:

'*Another sporting star involved in night-club brawl.*'

'*Sudden death of respected insect expert on West Uist.*'

147

The familiar inter-slot jingle sounded then:

'First we shall go straight to West Uist where earlier today I talked to local news editor, Calum Steele.

The photograph of Calum with slicked-down hair, bow tie and braces flashed up. Almost immediately there were hoots and laughter from around the bar.

'What have you done to your head, Calum? Stuck it in a vat of oil?'

'What's he wearing a ribbon around his neck for?'

'Look, he's wearing braces!'

Calum glared about him and waved his hands for silence as on the TV Kirstie asked him to give an account of the story. The audience quietened down and listened to the sombre tale.

'And I believe that there is some question of police negligence, Calum?' Kirstie asked pointedly.

'It has been rumoured, I am afraid,' came Calum's voice. 'The man was in police custody last night after being arrested for interrupting the TV show *Flotsam & Jetsam*.'

'Do you think that there could have been negligence, Calum?'

There was the sound of breath being drawn in, as if Calum was thinking hard before he answered. 'I would hate to think it. I know all of the local police on the island. The truth is that you have to keep an open mind. And then there was the question of the hammer.'

'Ah yes,' came Kirstie Macroon's voice. 'The hammer in question was a Highland hammer, for throwing that is?'

'Aye, it was PC Ewan McPhee's hammer. He is the champion hammer thrower of the Western Isles. His hammer was found in the blood-soaked pool just inches from Dr Dent's head.'

Kirstie Macroon's voice sounded pained. 'It didn't hit the poor man, did it?'

'I am assured not,' Calum replied.

'But it still begs many questions.'

'Indeed it does, Kirstie,' Calum replied.

There was another inter-slot jingle then the shot turned to Kirstie Macroon in the studio.

'And that was Calum Steele the *West Uist Chronicle* editor. We will be keeping in touch with Calum to keep you in touch with any developments on that story. And now for our next story we need to go over to Oban . . . '

The chatter in the bar started up again and Calum clapped his hands and turned to Cora. 'Well, that went rather well, I think. Come on lassie, I'll buy you a drink.'

But when he stood and turned towards the bar he was met by rows of frosty glowers and glares.

'What's the matter folks? Aren't you going to congratulate me on another scoop? Who'll have a drink with me?'

Mollie McFadden voiced the general mood of the bar. 'I think you and your lassie will be better drinking somewhere else, Calum Steele. You will not find many folk here wanting to drink with you.'

'No!' chirped in one of the regulars. 'Nor turn their back to you after the back-stabbing you just did on TV!'

6

I

Torquil clicked off the TV just as the *Flotsam & Jetsam* programme signature tune came on.

'Calum has really done it this time,' he said, taking a sip of his pre-dinner whisky. 'You would think he would have some sense of loyalty, wouldn't you, Uncle?'

Lachlan McKinnon had leaned forward to tug at the rubber bone that Crusoe had been gnawing away at by his feet.

'Och, you know Calum, Torquil. He won't have given it a moment's thought. He's so keen to sell stories he won't have thought that he could be dropping his friends in the mire.'

'It is Ewan and Morag that I am worried about. They are both sensitive in their own ways.'

'I take it there is nothing to be worried about? He was safe to be discharged?'

'I would back Morag's opinion every time. And the Drummonds agreed with her.'

'So what now? What is likely to happen?'

Torquil drained his glass and stood up.

'Right now, I think it is time to eat. Tomorrow I will have to see how I can take the sting out of the story. Calum seems to have precipitated things by getting the TV involved. It will hit the nationals as well, I expect.' He sighed. 'And, ultimately, it is all my responsibility. They were my officers acting on my behalf. I have a feeling it could get rather heavy going.'

Lachlan rose too and grinned as Crusoe jumped up, his tail wagging furiously as he held the rubber bone in his jaws as if trying to tease him.

'Aye, heavy is the head that wears the crown. It is the trouble with being in charge of anything.' He smiled and patted Torquil's shoulder. 'But at least you have Lorna's visit to look forward to soon.'

Torquil's mobile went off.

'Ah, I expect that is her,' he said with a grin. 'She said she would phone this evening.'

But, as he answered it, his face dropped and he grimaced at his uncle.

'Good evening, Superintendent Lumsden,' he said, in answer to the curt voice on the other end. 'Yes, I saw it.'

'And why was that the first I heard about it?' Superintendent Lumsden snapped.

'Because there was no immediate need for you to know, Superintendent.'

Torquil winced at the roar from the phone.

'Of course you should have bloody well told me, McKinnon! What is the matter with you? Why do I always have to hear about your cock-ups on Scottish TV news programmes?'

'If you will let me — ' Torquil began.

'Ah, now you want to tell me something, do you? Well, I want to tell you something, McKinnon. I am not happy. Not happy at all. That reporter chap seems to be on the button, which is more than I can say for you. Negligence, that is what he was inferring, you realize that, don't you?'

'There has been no negligence, Superintendent. I said — '

Superintendent Lumsden roared again. 'No negligence? Are you mad? A respected entomologist is found dead with a hammer by the side of his head. A hammer thrown by that buffoon of a constable of yours, and you say there is no negligence?'

'That is what I said, Superintendent.'

'And there was nothing negligent about letting him out of police custody just hours before he met his death?'

'Categorically not, Superintendent Lumsden. I take full responsibility for my officers.'

'That's what I wanted to hear you say, McKinnon. It is all your responsibility and if there was no negligence then there was incompetence. And that particular buck stops on your desk. Do I make myself clear?'

'As crystal, Superintendent.'

'Your desk, McKinnon. And that means it is your neck that is on the block.'

'Yes, sir, thank you for your support, sir.'

There was a momentary pause as if Torquil's superior officer was searching for a response.

'Well, that is all for now, McKinnon. I am glad that we had this little chat to clear the matter up. You know where we both stand. I want this story squashed as soon as possible otherwise you may be looking at a disciplinary.'

Torquil was about to reply, but the phone went dead in his hand.

Lachlan had diplomatically left the room to squat in the hall and stroke Crusoe. He straightened as Torquil came out of the sitting-room.

'Lumsden isn't pleased with me,' Torquil explained. 'He as good as said that if I put a foot wrong over this he'll have my guts for garters. You know how much he'd like to get rid of me.'

Lachlan shoved his hands deep in his pockets and frowned. 'I take it that means the responsibility does not go all the way up the chain of command?'

'No, I am the last link.'

'Did you ask him about Lorna?'

Torquil gave a rueful smile. 'It didn't seem an appropriate moment, Lachlan.'

II

Fergie was in a bad mood after the show that evening. After giving Geordie Innes and the crew a roasting for the way it had all gone, he grabbed Chrissie by the arm and flounced out.

'Where are we going, Fergie?' Chrissie asked.

'For a drink. Maybe four or five.'

'That's not a good idea, lover. You know it just makes black moods blacker.'

'Good. Then maybe I'll get into a proper dark mood and go and sort somebody out.'

Chrissie pulled him up and spun him round. She grabbed both his shoulders and looked him straight in the eye. 'Just what do you mean? Sort who out?'

Fergie's eyes seemed to be smouldering, as if he was full of rage. He stared back at her defiantly, and then in his best show biz manner he shrugged, smiled and kissed her on the cheek. 'Just a manner of speech, darling. I'm just peeved at that old fool Guthrie Lovat. He screwed my plans up

155

tonight. That show was like filming a jumble sale at the Wee Free. It wasn't exactly a barrel of laughs.'

Chrissie eyed him askance. 'You don't plan on getting drunk though, do you? You know I hate it when you get drunk.'

Fergie laughed. 'Why, because I get too boisterous?' Then he winked. 'Or is it because I don't get boisterous enough?'

She cuffed him playfully. 'Come on then. But let's just make it two drinks, and then go back for an early night.'

Fergie clicked his tongue. 'Agreed. Just enough alcohol to make me mildly frisky.'

They emerged on to Harbour Street and made their way towards the Bonnie Prince Charlie Tavern.

'I just hope that wee busybody of a journalist isn't there tonight,' Fergie whispered, as they approached.

'Calum Steele? Why, I thought you liked him?'

'He can give us publicity, Chrissie. I pretend to like him. He has his uses.'

Chrissie frowned. 'That's typical of you, isn't it, lover?' she said with just the trace of an edge in her voice. 'You have a talent for finding out how to use people.'

If he detected the edge he didn't show it. He grinned as he reached out to open the door of the Bonnie Prince Charlie Tavern. 'I do indeed, my darling. And it is that talent that keeps you in the style that you are used to.'

III

Calum Steele was seething with fury as he and Cora pushed open the door of the Commercial Hotel public bar.

'Can you believe it, Cora! Mollie McFadden asked me to leave! Me! The editor of the *West Uist Chronicle*.'

'And me, Calum. She asked us both to leave. I've never been thrown out of anything before. I don't know what Great-aunt Bella will say.'

At the mention of Miss Melville's name Calum felt a prickle at the back of his neck. 'Oh aye, that's a thought. What do you think she'll say?'

To his surprise Cora Melville let out one of her effervescent giggles. 'I have no idea, and to be honest, I don't care. It's all a bit of a laugh, isn't it? I mean, they all think we are the bad guys.' She tapped her chest with her thumb. 'Me — a bad guy. It's so exciting.'

Calum's eyes narrowed behind his spectacles. 'Oh, aye, I suppose it is quite. I mean, you get used to it.'

'And I guess it can be useful at times for a journalist. Being a social pariah, I mean.'

'A pariah? Actually, I wouldn't go as far as that, Cora. But you are right, it can be useful. Then when you make your next scoop they all think you are the bee's knees.'

'So we just need a scoop, eh, boss?'

Calum stood looking across the bar, seemingly oblivious to her last words.

'I said we just need a scoop — '

'Sh! I heard you, lassie. And I think we might just have stumbled on one. Just act naturally and follow me to the bar, then when we get there take a look at the group of men in the corner. You'll recognize one I am sure.'

They went to the bar and while Calum ordered drinks Cora casually looked around the bar, focusing as she did on the men drinking whiskies in the corner.

'I see what you mean, Calum,' Cora whispered, as she turned back to the bar to take the lemonade and lime that he pushed along the bar to her. 'There could be a scoop there all right.'

'Aye, that's what I thought.' He stroked his chin. 'We need to find out what the up-and-coming striker Sandy King is doing on West Uist.'

'Never heard of him, Calum. I thought you

meant Dan Farquarson, the biggest crook in Dundee. Him and his minder, Wee Hughie.'

Calum Steele almost choked on the first swig he took of his pint of Heather Ale.

IV

Guthrie Lovat's mobile phone went off.

He had been expecting the call. He took a gulp of the whisky and soda that he had just poured then waited a couple of further rings before he picked up the phone and pressed the answer button.

'Lovat here,' he said languidly.

'Christ! I thought you weren't going to answer. I tried you earlier and you didn't pick up.'

'I was beachcombing on the islands,' he replied. Then he said with a hint of sarcasm, 'You could have left a message.'

A hostile edge crept into the voice on the other end. 'Don't be bloody stupid! You know I never leave messages.'

'I know. So go on, talk to me.'

'There will be one tomorrow. Passing the rendezvous at three a.m. GMT. Usual jetsam.'

'And the usual payment?'

'Of course.'

He gritted his teeth at that. The whole bloody thing was starting to frustrate him. For a moment he considered trying to draw the guy out.

'Did you hear me?' snapped the voice. 'I said of course. The same payment and all the same arrangements.'

'I understand.'

The edge was there again. 'Just make sure you do. You know the penalty for non-compliance! It still applies.'

He swallowed hard. Part of him wanted to tell the voice to bugger off, but he knew that would be dangerous, suicidal perhaps. So instead he said, 'I know. And I love you too.'

This brought a humourless laugh then the phone went dead.

He stood looking at the dead phone for a moment before hurling it at the settee.

'One day, you bastard. One day!'

V

Morag heaved a sigh of relief when she finally got her three children to go to bed. Helping her youngest with homework had been an effort, for her mind had been preoccupied about the death of Digby Dent.

'Oh Morag Driscoll, what have you done?'

she moaned to herself, as she slumped on the settee with a large gin and tonic in her hand. She took a sip then screwed up her face in disgust.

'Ugh! Disgustingly bitter stuff that gin is,' she cursed, leaning forward and depositing the glass on the coffee table. 'Whatever was I thinking about trying to drown my guilty conscience in this filthy stuff that has been in a bottle for years? Sherry or fizzy white wine, that is your limit, you silly girl.'

She sat tapping the arm of the settee as she brought the previous evening's events back into her mind and replayed them.

Dent was as drunk as a lord, there was no mistaking that. A proper spectacle he made of himself on the TV show. She shook her head. Why ever would he do that? Drinking himself silly when he knew he was going to be on the TV. It was just so stupid.

Her mind went back to him coming into the station the day before to complain about Bruce McNab and his party.

He was not a very pleasant fellow, even when he was sober, though.

Then she thought about Sandy King and a slight smile came to her lips.

Now he is a much pleasanter chap altogether. Good-looking, a talented foot-baller and polite as well.

She sighed at the recollection of the interview she had with him, Bruce McNab and that Dundee businessman and his employee.

I wouldn't have minded having a drink with Sandy King on his own, she mused as her eye settled on the string of bubbles that rose from her unwanted gin and tonic. Her mind went off at a tangent and she leaned back and closed her eyes, imagining that she was reclining somewhere luxurious, with a glass of expensive champagne in her hand.

Maybe I could even grow to like —

The phone warbled in the corner and with a shrug of resignation she heaved herself to her feet.

'Don't worry girl,' she joked to herself. 'It is probably Sandy King ringing to ask you out for that drink.'

She was still smiling when she answered the phone.

'Morag, thank goodness I have got hold of you. It's me, Ralph McLelland.'

Morag suppressed a giggle and the urge to make a saucy joke. But Ralph McLelland was a doctor and sometimes he was just a tad old-fashioned, so she went straight into professional mode. 'And what can I do for you, Doctor?' she asked crisply.

'Was Dr Dent a bit of a junkie?'

'Afraid I have no idea. Any reason for asking?'

Ralph made a gruff noise as if he was irritated. 'I think I had better talk this over with Torquil. The trouble is that I just get an engaged noise when I call him. That's why I rang you.'

Morag sighed wistfully. 'No one ever calls me unless it is business, Dr McLelland. And maybe the reason you can't get hold of the inspector is because he is a man in love.'

'In love? What are you talking about?'

'Aye, he's in love with Sergeant Golspie. You remember? She's working at the station on Lewis. Superintendent Lumsden seconded her to work with the Customs. He's often on the phone to her at all sorts of pre-arranged times.'

'Ah! Stupid of me. I'll try him again. Bye.'

Morag stood looking at the receiver as he rang off. Talking about love had suddenly made her feel empty. Torquil was in love, just as she had been in love with her husband until that fateful day when he had his heart attack and died eight years before. Since then she had been both a mother and a father to her three kids.

'But right now I could do with a man in my life,' she said dreamily, as she replaced the receiver. 'Someone to help me out over this whole mess I have got myself into.'

The gin and tonic on the table started to look inviting.

She sat down and picked it up and then, closing her eyes, she took a hefty swallow.

VI

Torquil had been so glad to hear Lorna's voice after his conversation with Superintendent Lumsden. He was less happy to hear that the superintendent had just cancelled Lorna's next leave.

'The man is a miserable little piece of — ' he began.

'No need to say it,' Lorna interrupted. 'I agree, but we also both know that he has it in for us. Let's just take it on the chin for now. I'll be back soon enough.'

Torquil pulled a face. 'Just what is so important that he needs you there now?'

'It is important actually, love. A big Customs operation. He wants it to go well so he can add it to his CV.'

Torquil could barely disguise his contempt. 'Public-spirited of him, with other people's time.'

'It would be more Brownie points for him towards some honour or another. I think he is

164

hoping for an MBE or an OBE.'

'I would love to give him an honour,' Torquil said sourly. 'The grand order of the boot. And I would happily give it to him personally.'

Lorna laughed. 'Just make sure that your foot isn't inside the boot when you do, or he will have you for assault.'

They both laughed, and then fell into their usual exchange of endearments and lovers' talk.

The bleep on Torquil's phone went off to alert him that another caller had tried to ring him.

'Someone is being persistent,' he said between gritted teeth. 'But it could be an emergency so I had better go.'

Reluctantly they let each other go, then he pressed the answerphone function to find that Dr McLelland had left three increasingly terse messages. He called him straight away.

'Ralph, sorry I couldn't answer straight away, I was — '

'Torquil, I won't beat about the bush. I think I have bad news about Dr Dent?'

'Oh Lord! I was hoping it wasn't going to get any worse. I am worried about Morag as it is.'

'I just talked to her. But it wasn't her that I was concerned about.'

'Oh no, not Ewan then? Don't tell me that it was his hammer after all?'

Ralph growled irritably. 'If you would let me get a word in, Torquil! I have just finished his post-mortem and I am going through some of the laboratory work right now. I don't like what I am finding.'

'Tell me, Ralph.'

'Murder, Torquil. I think you have a murder on your hands.'

7

I

Calum had listened as Cora had whispered what she knew about Dan Farquarson and his dealings in Dundee. One of her tutors on the Abertay University journalism course had a second job on one of the Scottish dailies and had been involved in an undercover investigation into crime in the city. On a couple of occasions she had even gone drinking with him in a couple of the watering holes where some of the local bad boys hung out. She had even seen Farquarson and his main henchman, Wee Hughie. It was only an outline of the dealings that she had gleaned, but they were enough to make her cringe when she saw the two men in the corner of the bar.

'So what are we going to do?' Cora whispered to Calum, as they stood at the bar.

'Just wait until one of them comes to the bar to buy a round, then I'll engage them in conversation.'

Cora suppressed one of her giggles. 'Sorry, boss,' she said as he raised an eyebrow at her.

'I'm just a bit excited. It's like real journalism.'

'What do you mean *real* journalism?' Calum replied nonplussed. 'I'll have you know — '

But he did not finish the sentence for he had seen Bruce McNab gather a batch of empty glasses and start to move across the crowded bar. 'Watch me and wonder, lassie. Opportunity is on its way. First, we make room.'

And Cora watched as Calum casually straightened and turned, just as Bruce McNab approached the bar to give his order.

'Bruce!' Calum cried, as if greeting a long-lost friend. 'Why, fancy seeing you here. Come on, there's space here with me and my new reporter Cora Melville. Let me buy you a drink.'

Bruce McNab eyed Calum warily, then his eye set on Cora and he smiled. 'You are not related to Miss Bella Melville, are you, Cora?'

Cora shrugged her shoulders and smiled demurely. 'My great-aunt's reputation proceeds her everywhere I go.'

'Pleased to meet you,' Bruce said. Then, nodding at Calum, 'But I'll have to resist your kind offer, Calum, I'm with a party.'

'Oh aye,' Calum said, matter-of-factly, peering past Bruce as if seeing his party for the first time. 'Oh goodness me, is that Sandy King, I spy there?'

Bruce nodded to the barman and pointed to the empty glasses. 'Same again, Tam. And whatever Calum and Cora here would like.' As the drinks were being dispensed he placed a large hand firmly on Calum's shoulder. 'My clients are here on holiday, Calum. Do you know what I mean?'

'Oh aye, I know, Bruce,' Calum replied, tapping the side of his nose. 'Discretion. Don't worry, it's my middle name.'

'That's funny, Calum. Most folk around here think it is Nosy-Parker!'

Calum's cheeks reddened, but he said nothing. He merely grinned.

But this time Cora was unable to suppress one of her rippling giggles. It rose above the hubbub of the bar and almost every head turned to see the source of the laugh and to try to discern the cause of such hilarity. Wee Hughie stopped with his pint halfway to his lips and his eyes lit up. Seeing that Bruce McNab seemed to be having a joke with them he signalled them all over, much to Dan Farquarson's disdain.

'Hughie, what do you think you — ?' Dan Farquarson began, then seeing that Bruce McNab was returning from the bar with drinks, helped by the giggling girl and a short tubby fellow in a yellow anorak, he scowled and said in a short aside to Wee Hughie, 'We'll have words later, pal.'

But Wee Hughie gave no sign that he had heard his employer. He was on his feet immediately, pulling out a chair for Cora. 'Come away and sit down,' he cooed. 'Any friend of Bruce is a friend of mine. What was the joke?' He tapped her arm with his elbow. 'It wasn't anything smutty, I hope.'

Cora giggled again. 'Oh no, it was just that — ' She looked at Calum's raised eyebrows and then at Bruce McNab's stern mouth and hesitated. 'It was just something that my boss, Calum here, said. You tell them, Calum.'

'Well — ' Calum began.

'Calum Steele is our local newspaper editor,' said Bruce.

'A journalist?' queried Dan Farquarson, guardedly.

'Aye, Calum Steele, editor-in-chief of the *West Uist Chronicle*, at your service.' Despite himself, Calum's chest swelled slightly beneath his anorak. 'And this is Cora Melville, my — er — *cub* reporter.'

'A cub reporter, eh?' said Wee Hughie, unable to tear his eyes away from Cora. 'You mean like an assistant? Well, what I'd like to know is what's a bonnie lassie like you doing wasting your time on an island out here?'

'I am a Hebridean,' Cora replied immediately. 'I love the islands. I belong here.'

Wee Hughie grinned. 'Don't get me wrong, Cora, I like them myself. See, I think I like them more and more all the time.'

Calum took a seat next to Bruce and sipped his beer, then automatically wiped froth from his upper lip. He beamed at Dan Farquarson, then at Sandy King. His eyes opened wide with almost pantomimic effect and he clapped a hand to his mouth. Then as if recovering, he leaned across the table and asked, almost conspiratorially, 'Is it true? Am I really sitting at the same table as Sandy King, The Net-breaker?'

'That's me, all right,' Sandy replied. 'But I'm not looking for publicity. I'm just here for the fishing and hunting.' He grinned and slapped Bruce on the back. 'That's why we have engaged the services of the best fisherman on West Uist.'

Calum grinned. 'Aye, Bruce is famous around here. Not as famous as you of course, Sandy, but in West Uist he's a sort of celebrity.'

Bruce McNab frowned. 'That's havers, Calum, and you know it.'

'So, how was your fishing this morning?' Calum asked.

There was a moment of awkwardness as

the group looked at each other.

'We didn't get the fishing today,' said Dan Farquarson. 'We had a bit of a mix up. We didn't really meet up as we meant. So tomorrow we will make up for it. That's what we are doing now, you see. Planning tomorrow.'

'Do you like fishing, Cora?' Wee Hughie asked, staring at her dreamily.

Cora shivered. 'Ugh! I hate it. I am a strict vegetarian, you see. I couldn't possibly kill a fish.' She screwed up her face in distaste.

Wee Hughie looked bemused, but thought quickly. 'Actually, I'm not so keen myself. I'm just here with my boss.' He looked beseechingly at Dan Farquarson. 'I haven't had a bite at all, have I, boss?'

Dan Farquarson gave a humourless smile. 'No, nothing at all. He's useless, Cora. *Completely* useless.'

'Well — er — I wondered,' Calum said to Sandy, 'how would you feel about giving me a wee interview? The *West Uist Chronicle* readers would love to know what you think of our island.'

Dan Farquarson cleared his throat and Sandy King darted him a quick glance. It was not missed by either Calum or Cora.

'Look, Calum,' Bruce said, 'my clients are here for the fishing, not to be emblazoned across the front page of the *Chronicle*.'

'No need to include us in anything,' Dan Farquarson added. 'Wee Hughie and me are just here for the fishing, like Bruce here says. As for Sandy — '

'As for me, I can speak for myself,' Sandy King said firmly. Then he said to Calum, 'I'll give you an interview all right, Calum. But not here and not now. Tomorrow I'll call you. How's that?'

Calum produced a card with the skill of a conjurer and handed it over. 'Any time, Sandy. Day or night, the *Chronicle* reporters are always on hand.'

'Does that include you, Cora?' Wee Hughie asked with the hint of a leer.

Cora opened her mouth as if to give an indignant reply, but Calum answered for her.

'Oh, aye, that goes for all of the *Chronicle* staff!'

II

The lights were shining through the frosted glass of the Kyleshiffin Cottage Hospital mortuary as Torquil rode up. He dismounted and made his way through the outer doors, then pressed the intercom button and called his name.

Ralph McLelland's voice sounded almost

robotic through the speaker:

'Come straight through, Torquil. I'm in the lab.'

A buzzer sounded as the lock was released and Torquil pushed the door open and was immediately struck by the coppery odour of blood mixed with that of strong disinfectant. He walked past the closed post-mortem room door and tapped on the laboratory door at the end of the corridor before pushing it open.

Dr McLelland was dressed in blue surgical scrub clothes, sitting at a bench with a heap of notes on one side and several jars containing specimens of viscera on the other. In front of him was a microscope and various bottles of fixatives and stains.

'OK Ralph, so what have you come up with?'

'Questions, Torquil. Questions that don't make sense.'

'It's a bit late for riddles, Ralph. Tell me more.'

Ralph took a deep breath and sat back in his chair. He pointed at a jar containing pinky-grey tissue. 'This is Dr Dent's lung tissue. I've been looking at it. There is water in the lungs.'

'So he was drowned? That's what you expected, isn't it?'

'Yes — and no. That is, I expected to find water in his lungs, but not the type that shows up under the microscope.'

'The type of what, Ralph? The wrong type of water?'

'Exactly. He was found face down in a bog pool, right? In which case there should be bog water in his lungs. It should be brackish and teeming with algae and micro-organisms, like the specimen of water that I took when I examined the body *in situ*.' He tapped the microscope. 'But the water in his lungs is as clear as day. It is fresh water.'

'You mean it is river water?' Torquil asked with a puzzled look.

Ralph bit his lip. 'I'm not sure, except that it isn't the same as the water that he was found in.'

'Are you absolutely sure of that?'

'Pretty well sure. In order to be certain I would need to have a detailed chemical analysis done, which will take a few days as I'll need to send the specimens over to the Forensic Department at Dundee. I'll also be sending his blood off for toxicology as well, and, as you know, a detailed analysis can take a week or two.' He scratched his chin. 'But in the meanwhile there is another anomaly that makes Dr Dent's death seem decidedly fishy.' He stood up and signalled to the door. 'We'll need to have a look at the body.'

Torquil winced. 'Is he still — '

'Still open?' Ralph divined with a wry smile. 'No. I've done my work and sewn him up nicely so that any relatives can view the body. But it is his skin that I want to show you.'

Torquil followed him back to the post-mortem room. Although he had seen numerous dead bodies in his career, he still was not comfortable when he had to see post-mortems being carried out.

Ralph closed the door behind them then crossed to the raised marble slab in the middle of the room. He lifted the green sheet and pulled it back from the body to reveal the head and neck and the tell-tale T-shaped incision from shoulder to shoulder meeting above the sternum, then extending downwards. Ralph's neat suturing had united the ends of all of the skin edges leaving only two knots protruding; one at the end of the right-shoulder incision and the other at the T-junction where the two incisions met.

Despite himself Torquil found himself focusing on the sutures and the knots for a moment, rather than looking at the face of the corpse.

'You could have been a seamstress, Ralph,' he remarked casually.

Ralph McLelland gave a short laugh. 'Pah!

A frustrated surgeon I am. I always like to do as neat a job as I can for the relatives. And that includes my vertical mattress stitch and my one-handed surgical knots.'

Torquil nodded absently as he looked at Dent's face. It seemed so strange to think that just a short time before he had been full of life, lodging a complaint at the station.

'See his skin?' Ralph asked.

'What am I looking for, Ralph?'

'Midge bites. As you will see, there aren't any.'

Torquil thought back to the finding of the body. 'I remember Ewan remarked about that. There were no midges landing on him, whereas we were all being bitten to heck. You said that it was because Dr Dent was dead.'

'That's right. They are attracted to carbon dioxide given off by living, breathing creatures.'

'Then I don't see what you are getting at.'

'I was being stupid, Torquil. It is true that they don't bite, but they would have bitten him before he fell. I think the reason he doesn't have any bites is because he didn't die in that bog pool.'

'But he did drown?'

'Oh yes. He drowned all right, but not there.'

Torquil clicked his tongue. 'It is not looking good, Ralph. I think you are right. It looks like murder, right enough.' He shook his head. 'I have a bad feeling about this. There's something troubling me about what you've just shown me. Something that I just can't put my finger on.'

Ralph laid the sheet back over the body and nodded. 'That's weird, Torquil. I have that same feeling myself.'

III

Despite Cora's protests Calum had insisted on escorting her from the Commercial Hotel back to the *Chronicle* offices where he made up the camp-bed for her with fresh sheets and blankets.

'I'll feel safer about you here,' he explained. 'I was not liking the look of that big lad, Wee Hughie. He has his eye on you.'

'But I thought that was what you wanted, Calum?' Cora replied as she stood watching him with her arms across her chest. 'You told him that I was always on duty.'

'Of course I did. You are a carrot, Cora.'

'A carrot! Thanks very much, tattie head!'

'No, not a vegetable. The type that you dangle in front of donkeys to get them moving. There is a story here, my girl, and we're going to get on to it. Now, this is going to be good experience for you. A journalist has to get used to sleeping on the job. You get yourself settled, I'll grab a few cushions and I'll bed down in the archives room. You'll find new toothbrushes and toothpaste in the bathroom. In the morning we'll make a plan of campaign.'

He yawned, then went to the filing cabinet, pulled it open and took out his bottle of Glen Corlan whisky. 'I'll just have a wee dram to help me sleep. Would you like one?'

'Ugh!' Cora replied, screwing up her face in distaste.

'But whisky is OK for vegetarians,' he said encouragingly.

'I would rather drink engine oil. Good night, boss.'

Calum sighed as he stuffed a couple of cushions under his arm, grabbed a mug and made for the archive room. 'Good night, Cora.'

He was troubled. He wondered how she would cope in the cut and thrust world of journalism unless she developed a taste for Glen Corlan.

IV

The following morning Lachlan was up with the lark. As arranged the previous evening his plan was to meet the Reverend Kenneth Canfield at the church for prayers, then have a nine hole rematch before having a long discussion about a project concerning their ministries. He had left food for Crusoe and a note for Torquil, since he had retired the previous evening before his nephew had returned from his mysterious trip to see Ralph McLelland.

He saw Kenneth standing in the cemetery as he approached the church across the golf course.

'You are up bright and early, Kenneth,' he called, as he left his golf bag against the fence and pushed open the creaking wrought-iron gate into the cemetery.

'I was keen to talk to the Lord before I take my revenge.'

Lachlan struck a light to his pipe and joined him at the grave of Heather McQueen.

'It is a bit of a mystery who put these flowers on her grave,' he said, as he puffed his pipe. 'I mentioned it to my nephew.'

'Why did you do that?'

Lachlan was slightly taken aback at the tone in his colleague's voice. 'Oh just because he's a police officer and he deals in mysteries.'

'They are only flowers, Lachlan. I have a mind to put some on her grave myself.'

'It wasn't you that put these on?'

Kenneth Canfield's eyes seemed on the verge of watering. He stared at the flowers for a moment then shook his head. 'No. I have a suspicion who did though.'

'Oh! Who?'

'Digby Dent. I think he might have put them here out of guilt.' He smiled wistfully. 'I know a lot about guilt.'

'You were on the verge of saying something about that the other day, Kenneth. Is it something that you want to talk to me about now?'

Kenneth stared at his old friend. 'About Dr Dent? No, not just yet.'

'Or about guilt then?'

Kenneth gave a short laugh. 'Like a confession, you mean?'

'I am always here for that purpose, Kenneth, you know that.'

Kenneth patted his arm and wrinkled his eyes. 'Thank you for the offer, Lachlan. I appreciate it, but for now let's just go and say our prayers then let me get my revenge.'

Lachlan tapped out his pipe and ground the ashes in the gravel of the path. 'After you then.' He popped his pipe into his breast pocket and followed his guest. He felt slightly uncomfortable about the way that he had twice mentioned the word 'revenge'.

V

Cora had slept badly. Although the camp-bed was comfortable enough she had been unable to cut out the sound of Calum's snoring. When first light peeped through the shutters she rose, washed and dressed then searched the fridge and cupboards in search of breakfast. Finding only beer in the cupboard and a stack of mince pies and an assortment of things suitable for Calum's beloved frying pan she decided to simply have a cup of tea. Upon finding the tea caddy empty she pouted with disappointment and decided that the place needed some sensible restocking. She grabbed her bag and headed off for some fresh supplies.

At Allardyce's, she bought three butter rolls, a tub of low fat margarine and a small pot of honey. She positively skipped along Harbour Street enjoying the fresh sea air as she made her way to Anderson's Emporium to buy tea-bags.

It was already busy as an assortment of fishermen, yachts folk and nature-loving holidaymakers were buying supplies for the day.

She joined the queue and noted that there was only Agnes Anderson to serve all of the customers.

'What do you mean you have no

paracetamol?' a wiry young man in his late twenties complained to Agnes Anderson when it was his turn at the counter.

'I am sorry, sir, but we have had a run on them. You could always try the chemist. It will be open at nine o'clock.'

'Dash it! I haven't time to wait. Look, I don't like to ask this, but is there anything you can do? I just need about four of them. They aren't for me; they're for my bosses, Fergie and Chrissie Ferguson. They were — well, they were out having a drink or two last night.'

'I can vouch for that, Agnes,' a tall man standing behind them volunteered. 'I was in the Bonnie Prince Charlie. They bought everybody a drink. I was coming to buy some paracetamol for myself.'

There was communal laughter from the rest of the queue.

'I'll see what I can do,' said Agnes. 'Give me a minute and I'll raid our medicine cabinet.' She raised herself on tiptoe to address the rest of the customers. 'Sorry, folk, I'll get to you all as soon as I have taken care of this gentleman.'

When she had left, Geordie turned to the queue. 'I apologize for this, ladies and gentlemen. That's show-biz folk for you, I'm afraid. But please, don't let anyone know that

I was in here for this. You know what the media are like. A pack of animals the lot of them.'

The tall man was quick to agree. 'Aye, and we have a real wee Rottweiler of a newshound here on West Uist. Calum Steele the editor of the *Chronicle* would hang out his own granny's dirty washing if it sold more copies of his rag.'

'He's more of a Jack Russell in my opinion,' chirped in someone else, much to the amusement of the rest.

'I know the man,' Geordie Innes confided. 'You should hear what Fergie calls him.'

And, as the other customers joined in the ragging of Calum Steele, Cora felt her hackles rise. Part of her wanted to wade in to defend her boss, but the other part told her to keep her head down. No one knew that she was a member of his staff and that could be useful. She listened as Geordie Innes let one or two little nuggets of gossip about the *Flotsam & Jetsam* show slip out, much to the glee of the emporium customers.

As the shop gradually cleared and she took her turn at the counter, Agnes Anderson smiled at her.

'Are you on holiday, miss?' she asked.

'No, I've moved here for a while.'

'Working here are you?'

Cora began to feel uncomfortable with the

questioning. It was time to be evasive. 'Sort of. I'm a writer of sorts.'

'Really? Are you writing a novel then?'

'Well, I'm thinking about it. That's why I need more tea.'

Agnes tittered. 'Oh mercy me, there I go being a Nosy Parker. Sorry, miss. Is it a small box or a big box you want?'

'Your largest. You have no idea how much tea — ' She stopped herself just in time, for she had been about to mention Calum's name. She grinned, then added, 'That I drink while I'm doodling.'

She couldn't wait to tell Calum about the nuggets she had collected. And, as she walked back to the *Chronicle* offices, she realized that there was something very exciting about being an investigative journalist. She could quite see why it all gave Calum a buzz.

Yet her image of Calum Steele, editor-in-chief and investigative journalist *par excellence* took a sudden dip as she bounced up the stairs with her supplies.

The toilet door was open and Calum, dressed in underpants and a string vest, was kneeling over the toilet retching into the bowl.

He pushed himself up and looked round at the sound of her footsteps. His hair was lank and his face was as pale as the porcelain of the toilet bowl that he was clutching.

'Ah, Cora, I wondered where you were. We had better sit down and plan our next move.' He hiccupped. 'I'm not feeling so great today. I think I might have eaten a few too many nuts at the pub last night. My tummy is a wee bit upset.'

Cora refrained from making any comment about the whisky that he had taken to bed. Instead she offered to make him tea with a butter roll and honey.

She winced as he shook his head and sank his head in the toilet to retch again. A moment later he heaved himself up and looked round with a pleading grin.

'Do you think you could pop round to Anderson's Emporium and ask them for some paracetamol?'

'Oh really, Calum!' Cora cried in exasperation.

VI

Ewan had been for his early morning run and a spot of hammer practice before opening up the station. He was busily working his way through the backlog of cases when Morag came in. One look at her and he lifted the counter flap and took her arm.

'Morag, what's wrong? You look like death

warmed up. Shall I get you something?'

'A paracetamol and a cup of your strong tea would be wonderful,' she said with a wan smile. 'And anything you have for guilt.'

'Och, Morag!' Ewan exclaimed. 'You have nothing to be guilty about. Everyone has told you that. It was me who wasn't looking where I was throwing my hammer.'

'Oh you are a wee darling, Ewan. But it isn't just that I feel guilty about. I drank too much last night. I was on my own after I had put the kids to bed. It is something I have never done before.' She clenched her fists until her nails dug into her palms. 'It was so irresponsible of me.'

Ewan patted her shoulder. 'No one will think the worse of you for that, Morag. Now go and have a seat in the rest room and I'll bring tea and a paracetamol through to you.'

No sooner had he performed that duty than the station bell tinkled and the first client of the day came in. It was Rab McNeish.

'Ah, Mr McNeish,' Ewan greeted him warmly, belying his real feeling of dread as he expected another tirade of invective amid the inevitable complaints about cats and dogs.

But it never came. Instead, the undertaker looked somewhat sheepish.

'I — er — I need to report something.'

Ewan picked up his pencil and licked the

tip. 'Fire away then, Mr McNeish. I am all ears. What is the complaint?'

'It's not a complaint, it's a report I am making. About a theft. I have been robbed, sort of.'

'At your house, you mean? You live out on Sharkey's Boot, don't you?'

'Aye. Well, really all I need is a crime number for my insurance company.'

'I just need some details first Mr McNeish. Then I can call round on Nippy sometime this morning.'

'There's no need for that, it's just a number they say.'

'Well, what's been stolen?'

'Oh just a few bits of antiques. Nothing grand.'

'Funny that. I've got a few cases of burglary on the books at the moment. Antique clocks, old knick-knacks, that sort of thing. You must be the — '

The bell tinkled again and the door opened to the sound of several dog barks. This was immediately followed by the entrance of Annie McConville in her usual panama hat, cheesecloth dress and a pack of assorted dogs on leads.

'Ah PC Ewan McPhee, the very man,' she said, advancing to the counter. Then she saw Rab McNeish, standing rigidly in front of

188

her, both hands clutching the edge of the counter. 'Ah, and as for you, Rab McNeish, I want a word with you! You've been spreading rumours and making complaints about me, I hear.'

It was as if the dogs all noticed him for the first time as well, and two of them bared their teeth, barked and made a lunge at him. Annie immediately tugged their leads and Zimba, her German shepherd put himself between the two small dogs and the joiner.

'Wheesht, boys!' she called and they instantly quietened, but stood glaring menacingly at the now stricken Rab McNeish.

Ewan sensed the possibility of conflict and tried to intervene. 'I'll be with you in a moment, Mrs McConville. I was just dealing with Mr McNeish.' He turned to the joiner-cum-undertaker. 'So would you like to give me the details of these antiques?'

'Er — no! I've changed my mind. They're not worth claiming. Not now. Not yet. I'll — er — I'll maybe come back.'

He edged round the dogs.

'I won't take kindly to hearing any more tittle-tattle, you know,' Annie went on. 'If you have something to say to me, say it instead of going scuttling about behind my back.'

Rab McNeish bobbed his head up and down and made a dash for the door.

'But, Mr McNeish,' Ewan began.

'Oh don't bother your head about him, Ewan McPhee. He's just a scunner and a troublemaker.' She slapped her hand on the counter. 'Now, I have a clue for you.'

'A clue, Mrs McConville?'

'Yes, about the case of the abandoned cats and dogs that you are investigating.'

'Er — are we?'

'Of course you are! Miss Melville reported it all to Sergeant Morag Driscoll. Don't tell me that you don't know.'

Ewan considered that discretion would be the best option. 'So what is this clue, Mrs McConville?'

'They don't like the sound of a saw. I have four of them that just cower away.'

'I don't understand you, I am afraid.'

'I get spare shanks from Mathieson, the butcher. I saw them up for my doggies so that they all get good marrow and plenty of calcium. Well, they all start howling and then they just cower away into corners as if there's a thunderstorm going on.' She stared at Ewan who was uncertainly chewing the end of his pencil. 'Well, write it down then, it could be crucial to the case. Tell Sergeant Morag. Good day to you.'

And without more ado she flounced out with her pack of animals leaving a bemused

Ewan to add her information to the day record. He would marry it up with the case which he was sure would be in the backlog.

He was still writing when the bell tinkled again and Sandy King came in, dressed in a plain black track suit.

'Are — are you — ?'

'Sandy King, that's right. I just wondered if I could have a quick word with Sergeant Driscoll.'

'I'll see if I can find her,' Ewan said, and turned to find Morag coming in.

'Did I hear my name mentioned,' she asked. Then she saw the footballer and colour appeared in her cheeks.

'It's a personal matter, actually,' he said, looking meaningfully at Ewan.

'Oh, I'll just put the kettle on, Sergeant Driscoll,' Ewan said, leaving diplomatically.

'I've been plucking up courage, Morag,' Sandy King said. 'Is it OK to call you that? I just thought maybe we could have that drink I mentioned the other day. Just you and me.'

'I — er — would love to,' she said. 'When I'm off duty.'

His smile enchanted her. 'That's settled then.' He handed her a card. 'My mobile is on there. Just ring when you are free. Look I need to rush, myself. I have another appointment to keep. Look forward to our date.'

Morag stared at the door as it closed behind him. 'I don't believe it,' she said to herself.

'Ewan,' she called through to the kitchen. 'Am I dreaming or not? Did Sandy King just come in?'

'He did, and he asked you out on a date.'

'Were you listening, you big galoot?'

'Of course I was, and I'm happy for you. Could you get his autograph for me, or maybe a football shirt?'

There was a chorus of laughter from the rest room and the Drummond twins appeared, both of them dressed in the West Uist police navy-blue jumpers.

'Special Constables Wallace and Douglas Drummond reporting for duty, Sergeant Driscoll,' said Wallace. 'We just came in the back door in time for tea and heard the good news too.'

'You'll be asking Torquil for a holiday then,' said Douglas with a grin.

The bell tinkled again and Torquil himself came in with Crusoe trotting loyally at his feet.

'Did I hear someone mention the word holiday?' Torquil asked, as he lifted the flap and let himself in. 'I'm afraid there will be no holiday leave for a while folks. We've got a murder investigation to set up.'

8

I

Ewan made a huge pot of tea and distributed mugs to the team as they sat around the rest room listening to Torquil's news.

'Ralph McLelland is still conducting tests, but it is conclusive enough already to know that there has been foul play.'

Morag stared at him in disbelief. 'So it is definitely murder? No mistake?'

'Foul play, Morag,' said Torquil as he absently stroked Crusoe who was lying contentedly at his feet. 'It looks like murder, but that is not absolutely certain. What is certain is that he didn't die on Kyleshiffin moor. His body was dumped there.'

'Aye, I see what you mean,' said Wallace. 'Why would someone move the body if he hadn't been murdered?'

'But where was he killed?' Douglas asked. 'And why was he moved?'

'That's what we need to find out,' said Torquil. 'But so far we know next to nothing about him, apart from the fact that he was an entomologist here studying midges.'

'He was a drinker,' said Ewan. 'He ruined that TV show, *Flotsam & Jetsam*, and he spent time in the cell.' He patted Morag's shoulder. 'And if it is murder, then it lets all of us off the hook.'

'Maybe, Ewan,' Torquil replied. 'But he would have been safe while we held him. Someone may have been waiting for him to be discharged.'

Ewan beetled his brows. 'Och, but we didn't know that. Surely the Press won't keep up that tack?'

'By the Press, did you mean Calum Steele?' Wallace asked. 'That wee toad has shown that he'd do anything for a story.'

'So are you going to tell him, boss?' Douglas asked.

'I haven't thought about that yet,' Torquil replied. He bit his lower lip. 'The first person I need to talk to is our esteemed Superintendent Lumsden. I tried to ring him last night after I found out from Ralph, but his wife said that he was out and she had no way of getting a message to him. She was all hush-hush about it. She said she was expecting him this morning at nine.'

Morag shook her head. 'That man is not right in the head, I am thinking. He wants to know all that is happening, but he makes himself unavailable when something important comes up. It's almost as if he knows how to make matters difficult for us.'

'For me, you mean, Morag,' Torquil corrected with a wry grin. 'It occurred to me as well, but then I thought that's just me being paranoid. How could he know anything about this? No, I'll ring him in a minute and then we'll go through the backlog of cases that need looking at, decide what can be held and divvy out the tasks to get this investigation on the road.'

He got up and headed towards his office. 'I'll get this over with now. Ewan, you get the case book and Morag can start going through it while I fill Superintendent Lumsden in.'

II

Cora was amazed at the speed with which Calum seemed to recover.

'I told you, it was something I ate,' he explained, as he tucked into a cold mutton pie. 'I just needed to pump up the stomach contents and I knew I'd be fine.'

'But why are you filling it up with that disgusting thing? Don't you feel sick?'

'Not now,' Calum returned, wiping a trickle of cold grease from his chin then taking a hefty gulp of tea. 'Cora, you have a lot to learn about journalism, but stick with me and I'll teach you all you need to know. You may not think it, but I know exactly how to handle my stomach and what is good for it. Now, as for you and all that veggie stuff, do you really — ?'

His mobile phone went off and he promptly answered it. 'Hello, yes, Calum Steele speaking.'

Cora watched as his eyes turned into big round orbs to mirror the shape of his spectacles. 'Sandy! Great to hear from you. Of course, one o'clock would be terrific. Excellent, I'll see you there.' He went silent for a moment, nodded his head, and then winked at her. 'Wee Hughie asked that?'

He made a thumbs-up sign at her. 'Oh I'll pass that message on to her, but I can't give out her phone — ethics, you know. But between us, I think she'd be delighted to see him. Tell him she'll be there.'

Cora's eyes went wild and she clenched her fists at him.

'OK, Sandy. I'll see you here at one o'clock and I'll pass that message on to Cora.'

He snapped his phone shut and tossed it on to the desk before taking another mouthful of pie. 'See, it's all working out smoothly, Cora. Sandy King is going to come here for an interview with me at one.'

'I heard that. And what was that about me? Me and that ape, Wee Hughie? What did you

196

mean, I'd be delighted to see him?'

'Apparently he's smitten. Couldn't stop talking about you last night. He's asked that you meet him at one o'clock in the Commercial Hotel for a lunchtime drink.'

'Oh Calum!'

'What? Our plan worked, didn't it?' He winked. 'Just like I thought it would. Now, look, I'm going to follow up on Sandy King and why he is here, and you are going to have lunch and find out as much as you can about what this hoodlum and his boss are doing on West Uist.'

'But wouldn't it be better if I did the Sandy King investigation?' Cora asked pleadingly.

Calum winked at her over the rim of his mug. 'Ah, the trouble is, Wee Hughie doesn't fancy me.'

III

'Well, Superintendent Lumsden was a delight, as usual,' Torquil said as he returned to the rest room after his phone conversation with his superior officer.

'He wasn't pleased, was he?' Morag asked, rhetorically.

'A bit less than usual,' Torquil returned. 'He wants to be kept in the loop and he wants results yesterday.' He clapped his hands. 'So come on, folks, let's get started. First of all, let's have a run down on what we have on the book.'

Morag quickly ran through the cases, giving a thumbnail description of each and what stage each case was at. She and Ewan added about their respective chats with Annie McConville.

'So really,' she said at last, 'the way I see it, we have seven burglaries of assorted antiques, family knick-knacks, a couple of computer thefts, then there was the break-in at the *Chronicle*. And, of course, there is this dog and cat business.'

At the mention of this Crusoe momentarily lifted his head and wagged his tail a few times before lying down again and closing his eyes.

'He's just showing that he's on the ball,' Torquil grinned. 'But although this murder investigation must take priority, we can't let these other things slip.' He turned to the big constable.

'Ewan, you can do a bit of following up on the burglaries to show that we've made a start and are taking home crime seriously.'

'Aye that's it, Torquil. Give the big lad a bit of air. He fairly likes gadding about the island on his mum's old Nippy moped,' Wallace teased.

'I'll give you gadding about, Wallace Drummond,' Ewan retorted.

'Do you want us to look into this cat and

dog affair then, boss?' Douglas asked.

Torquil considered for a moment then shook his head. 'No, I think that Crusoe and I will take a closer look at that when we have the time. It feels personal ever since he came to live with us.'

'So it's the *Chronicle* case then?'

Again Torquil shook his head. 'No, I started that and I'll keep it under my wing, too. But we'll let him stew a little bit, I think.' Then he grinned. 'It will be good for him. Besides, I have another idea to teach the wee man a lesson.' He clapped his hands and stood up abruptly. 'In fact, no time like the present. I'll just pop through to my office for a couple of minutes, and then we'll pool all the information we have about Dr Dent's murder. Ewan, get the whiteboard ready, will you?'

Ewan wheeled the whiteboard that they used for major cases to the end of the room while the twins moved the table tennis table that they used for occasional recreation against the wall. Morag got out fresh ink markers and laid out paper and pencils for note making. By the time they had the room ready for the meeting Torquil had come back rubbing his hands with glee. Crusoe trotted loyally at his heels.

'You look pleased, boss,' said Douglas.

'Fairly. Let's just say that phase one has

gone smoothly. Now let's get cracking.'

Torquil picked up a marker and went to the whiteboard. In the middle he wrote DR DIGBY DENT and surrounded it with a circle. Then he added underneath: MURDERED, HEAD INJURY, DROWNED.

And underneath that BODY BEEN MOVED.

'OK, brainstorming time. What do we know?'

'He was the midge man,' said Morag.

'He was rude,' added Ewan.

'He got drunk on that TV show,' Douglas volunteered.

Wallace glanced at Morag, and then said, 'He was arrested and held here until he sobered up.'

'I found him up on the moor,' Ewan said mournfully, his face going pale at the thought. 'My hammer was just inches from his head and I thought I had killed him.'

Torquil held up his hand. 'OK, that's enough now. Let me get this all down.'

He began making one line notes of all the suggestions so far under the name of Dr Dent, then to the left he wrote FLOTSAM & JETSAM and enclosed it in a square. Underneath it he wrote the names Fergie and Chrissie and circled each.

'He was rude, as Ewan says. And he came in here to complain about Bruce McNab and his fishing and hunting clients.'

To the right of Dr Dent's name he wrote FISHING PARTY, put it in a square, and then underneath drew four lines. Under the first he wrote Bruce McNab, circled it, under the second added Sandy King and circled it as well.

'Who were the others, Morag?'

Morag checked her notes of the meeting she had. 'Mr Dan Farquarson and Hugh Thompson. They called Thompson Wee Hughie, which is a bit of a misnomer, since he's built like a proverbial.'

Torquil added the names and circled them, adding Morag's details underneath. He looked over at her and noticed the blush that had crept into her cheeks. 'Are you all right, Morag? You look flushed.'

'Ah, that's love, boss,' said Douglas. 'Tell him, Morag.'

'Tell me what?' Torquil asked.

'I — er — I have been asked out for a drink by Sandy King. Is that a problem, do you think?'

Torquil stared at her for a moment then shrugged. 'I don't see any problem, except he is on this board.'

'But he's not a suspect, is he, Torquil?' Wallace queried.

'We haven't got as far as making anyone a suspect, Wallace. But we just need to bear this in mind.' He clicked his tongue. 'Who knows?

It might even be useful.'

He turned his attention to the board again. 'It isn't a lot to go on, is it? We'll need to check things out with the University of the Highlands.' And so saying he added U of H to the notes underneath the name of Dr Dent.

'Which reminds me,' he said after a moment, 'the Reverend Kenneth Canfield is on the island at the moment. He's one of Lachlan's golfing chums. He is the chaplain at the university.' He added his name and circled it. 'I'll have a word with Lachlan and see if he knows anything of interest.'

'Did Dr Dent have any relatives?' Morag asked.

'Not that I know of. Ralph McLelland contacted his GP and as far as they know he was a man on his own. No parents, no siblings, no cousins.'

'So where do we go from here, boss?' Wallace asked.

'We gather as much information as we can. So let's divvy things up. First we need to find out all that we can about Dent. I think that will mean a bit of phoning about. Morag that's your forte, isn't it?'

Morag pouted. 'How did I guess you were going to say that?'

'You know me, I think,' Torquil replied. 'Just as Wallace and Douglas know what I'm going to ask them to do.' He looked expect-antly at them.

'It will be the heavy job,' Wallace replied.

'Or the dirtiest job,' Douglas added. 'But go on, boss, tell us. We're up for anything.'

'It's not dirty and shouldn't be hard either,' Torquil returned. 'I need you lads to go and check out Dent's cottage. We just need to know that the place is secure.'

'We can do that,' Wallace said. 'But what about Sherlock Holmes over there?' he said, grinning at Ewan. 'Isn't he going to be given something to test his mettle?'

'I'll test your mettle, you long drip of — '

'Ewan! Don't rise to the bait,' Torquil said calmly. 'You've got an important series of jobs to do.'

'Name it Torquil. I am keen to get whoever did this thing.'

'It isn't the Dr Dent case, Ewan. As I said, I want you to go and make a start with these burglaries. Then once we've got things up and running and we know a bit more about Dr Dent then you can come on board with the murder investigation.'

Ewan's expression showed his disappoint-ment, but he straightened. 'Of course, sir. Whatever you say.'

'And what are you going to do, Torquil?' Morag asked.

Torquil reached down and scratched Crusoe's head. 'I am going to make a start on this cat and dog business. I am going to see Annie McConville first, then I am going to see if I can catch up on Uncle Lachlan to see if I can get hold of the Reverend Kenneth Canfield.'

He glanced at his watch. 'Let's aim to meet back here at lunch, and then we'll see where we go next.'

IV

Ewan made his way along Harbour Street on Nippy. The street was busy with both the market-stalls on the sea-wall side and the multi-coloured shops doing a brisk trade.

He was feeling a little peeved at being kept out of the murder investigation, especially since the Drummond twins had been given a job that he felt he, as the regular constable, should have been given.

'Och! And they are just special constables,' he muttered under his breath. 'Sometimes I think Torquil goes a bit easy on them because of that.'

But in a way he was pleased to have been given the other task. After all, he knew that despite his size he had a squeamish side and the memory of finding Dr Dent's body face down in the bog-pool had kept coming back to him.

'That cheeky streak of nonsense called me Sherlock Holmes! They think they are so much smarter than me. Well, I'll show them. I'm going to solve some of these burglaries and then I'll make them laugh on the other side of their faces.'

He opened up the throttle and peddled hard to give the moped more power to get up the hill.

'We'll start with old Mrs Rogerson at Aberstyle Farm. She sounded upset at the theft of her grandfather's tobacco tin collection.'

He took the road that skirted Kyleshiffin moor and breathed deeply, enjoying the salty, peaty air. Then he swerved when he saw the dark haze rising from bushes at the side of the road.

'Blasted midges!' he cursed.

He did not notice the glint of sun on the lenses of a pair of binoculars that were trained on him.

V

Annie McConville always amazed Torquil. Although she was in her late seventies she seemed to thrive on hard work and was always on the go. Her animal sanctuary was famous throughout the islands and she was regarded as something of a local celebrity.

She was scuttling about with a wheelbarrow of straw, busily cleaning out the cat cages in the outhouses while Torquil followed her. Crusoe was tagging along behind him on his lead, while Zimba her German shepherd and Sheila her West Highland terrier lay on the floor wagging their tails.

'So how many strays have you actually had recently, Annie?'

Annie turned and straightened. 'Too many by far. Six dogs and three cats. I can't understand it. We've never really had a problem on the island before.' She scowled. 'No matter what that scunner Rab McNeish may say.'

'Oh, what does Rab say?'

'You know very well, Inspector McKinnon. The man is not right in the head. He has a thing about germs. He has been spreading malicious rumours about me and my dogs. He thinks that whenever a dog fouls any patch of ground it is me and one of my animals that is at fault.'

Torquil nodded. 'I was aware that he had mentioned some such thing.'

Annie waved a brush under his nose and

Torquil stepped back adroitly.

'Well, he will not do it again. I told him myself this morning at the station.'

'You were at the station this morning?'

'Goodness me! Do those folk that you work with not tell you anything? I was in telling Ewan McPhee an important piece of information. I am surprised that he hasn't told you.'

'Well, we — er — have a rather important investigation on at the moment, Annie.'

'Oh, and what sort of investigation is more important than the welfare of these waifs and strays?'

'I am not at liberty to say just at this moment, Annie. But what was this information?'

'It was about sawing bones. None of the stray dogs likes it.'

'I don't follow you.'

Annie tut-tutted. 'Well, look, the easiest thing is for me to show you. Come through to the kitchen.'

And she led the way to another outhouse which had been tiled inside so that it was clinically clean. She went and scrubbed her hands, then opened a fridge freezer and took out a couple of marrow bones. She deposited them on a wooden chopping board on a strong bench.

'We'll just leave the door open. They'll all hear well enough.'

And producing a long saw she started sawing one of the bones.

Almost immediately a chorus of howls and yelps rang out from the cages in the lower outhouses.

'They don't like it, you see,' Annie said. 'What do you make of that, Inspector McKinnon?'

'Not a lot, Annie,' Torquil replied. 'Zimba and Sheila are barking away as well. Maybe it is just something that dogs don't like.'

'Och, will you not listen properly? Zimba and Sheila are telling the others to hold their wheesht. They are the seniors, you see. All the others are howling in distress. They don't like it. Listen now, I'll do it again.'

And as if on cue the yelping and howling started up again as soon as the rasping of metal on bone rang out.

This time Torquil noticed that Crusoe was also whimpering. Not only that, but he was shaking, as if with fear.

'Goodness, Annie, you are right. Just look at Crusoe here.' He knelt down and stroked the dog's head.

'Poor thing,' she said, kneeling as well. And at her touch, her almost mystical touch with animals, Crusoe calmed down. He looked at her with his ears tucked back and licked her outstretched hand.

'It is clear to me, Inspector. All of these poor animals have been scared. Mistreated they have been.'

'I will find out who did this, Annie,' Torquil vowed. 'It is sounding as if it is one person who is at the bottom of it. Whoever it was tried to murder Crusoe here.'

And he recounted about how he had found Crusoe at St Ninian's Cave, lashed to a piece of timber.

'Could he have been thrown from a boat, do you think?' Annie asked.

'I have no idea, actually. It could have been from a boat or he could have been tossed in somewhere along that coast and drifted.'

Annie bit her lip as she thought. 'You might do worse than have a word with Guthrie Lovat. He must know more than anyone about the way flotsam and jetsam drift on to the beaches round here.' She shrugged her shoulders. 'If he will let you in to see him that is.'

'I don't think I have ever actually talked to him,' Torquil mused.

'Aye, well, he keeps himself to himself. And he's not an animal lover, that I can tell you.'

'Really?'

'Aye, really. Years ago before he had made his money and bought that strip of beach at Half Moon Cove, I used to walk the dogs there. They used to love to have a run over the sands. But that Guthrie Lovat saw us one time and started pelting the dogs with stones. I gave him a good ticking off.'

Torquil stood up. 'Thank you for that, Annie. I'll certainly consider it. It's probably time that I got to know our famous beachcombing artist.'

VI

Wallace and Douglas drove up the old dirt track towards Dr Dent's cottage. Wallace drew their battered pick-up truck to a halt just before the wooden gates beyond which Dr Dent's aged Land Rover was parked.

'It's a bit weird calling at the house of a dead man,' Wallace remarked.

'Especially when it looks like he was murdered,' Douglas agreed.

They let themselves through the wooden gate and crunched up the gravel drive.

'Dr Dent doesn't seem to have been one for gardening then,' Douglas said, pointing to the overgrown garden with knee high grass and weeds.

Wallace shrugged. 'Why would he be? It isn't as if he owned the place. Morag says it was rented on his behalf by the University of the Highlands.'

'You can hardly see that pond for all the grass,' Douglas replied with a nod towards a fish pond with several large goldfish visible under a surface carpet of water lily leaves.

The front door was locked and the windows were all closed.

'Let's check the back,' Douglas suggested, leading the way.

It only took a few moments to do a circuit of the cottage.

'It seems secure enough,' Douglas pointed out as he shielded his eyes and peered through a front window. 'But it's a bit of a mess inside.'

'I see what you mean,' his brother agreed, as he joined him at the sill and looked in.

Through the glass they saw that the front room had been arranged as a sort of laboratory. There were various electronic gadgets and an assortment of glass apparatus stacked on a table, with a microscope and an array of chemical bottles and fixatives. It seemed untidy to say the least.

A bookcase against a back wall looked as if someone had pulled every book out of it and thrown them higgledy-piggledy on the settee.

'Look at that great wet area over by that box thing.'

'That's not a box, Douglas,' Wallace corrected. 'It's some sort of tank with pipes attached to it.'

The twins looked at each other.

'Are you thinking what I am thinking, Wallace?'

Wallace swallowed hard and nodded. 'I think so. I don't know why he would have a tank of water in his front room, but he was a scientist. An odd one at that! But Dr Ralph McLelland said he was drowned, but not where he was found on the moor.'

'We'd better let Torquil know pretty damned quick. He might just have been murdered in his own cottage.'

VII

Morag had been on the telephone non-stop since the others had gone off on their various tasks.

First she telephoned Ralph McLelland and ascertained what personal effects of Dr Dent's he had in his possession. And, of course, she asked him for a résumé of his findings, so that she could start organizing the case file.

Calling the University of the Highlands

had resulted in her being directed to various people including the university chancellor, the head of the department of biological sciences and then to the HR department. All of them had been shocked to hear of Dr Dent's death, but were even more shocked to discover that the police thought that his death was suspicious.

She talked with Jenny Protheroe, the HR director, who gave her as much information as they had on Dent. That merely amounted to a run through his curriculum vitae, which she agreed to scan and send over by email, and an acknowledgement that he was alone in the world with no known relatives.

'I can't say that I liked the man,' Jenny confessed. 'He had a reputation, you see.'

'A reputation? What sort of reputation, Jenny? Any information could be relevant.'

There was a moment's hesitation. 'He was a Lothario.'

'A Lothario? You mean he liked the ladies?'

'And how! Staff, students, anyone in a skirt, if you know what I mean.'

Morag noted the tone of bitterness in her voice and wondered whether Jenny Protheroe, director of HR at the university had been targeted at some stage.

'Was he in a relationship recently, do you know?'

'Not that I know of. Women were wary of him ever since last year. One of his students, Heather McQueen drowned when she was doing post graduate work with him on West Uist.'

'Ah, of course. A tragedy.'

'There were rumours about an improper relationship.'

'But nothing like that came out at the Fatal Accident Inquiry,' Morag remarked.

'Well, it wouldn't, would it?'

Morag made careful notes of the conversation and then made a list of bullet points to tell Torquil.

She was just about to phone Ewan to ask him to collect Dr Dent's effects from the mortuary when she opened her diary and she saw Sandy King's card inside the cover. She felt her cheeks warm and she smiled.

Before she knew what she was doing she had dialled his number. The call was answered even before she had time to change her mind.

'Sandy King here.'

'Oh — er — it's Morag Driscoll.'

'Hi, Morag, I am glad you rang. When are you free?'

'It's not so easy to say, er — Mr King, you see — '

'My name is Sandy.' She noticed the

214

amusement in his voice.

'Sorry — Sandy! It's the police training. The formality, I mean.'

'I was kind of hoping that I could get behind that. Find the informal Morag.'

Morag's hand went to her hair and she started twirling a strand. Goodness, what am I doing here, she thought? I'm like a wee girl. I should just pull the plug before this gets out of hand.

'Maybe you can,' she heard herself say. She hesitated and then added, 'I have to tell you that I was married. I am a widow.'

'So I believe.'

'And I have three kids.'

'I know. I found that out for myself.'

'And you still — ?'

'I really want to meet up with you, Morag. So, when can we fix it?'

She paused for a moment, then: 'Tonight at eight. I'll get my sister to baby-sit. Meet me at Arbuckle's; it's a little wine bar-cum-restaurant just off Deuglie Street which you'll find at the top of Harbour Street. We can get a glass of wine or a beer.'

'A meal sounds good to me. Eight o'clock it is. I can't wait. Bye, Morag.'

'Bye — Sandy.'

Morag stared at her mobile in disbelief. Was it true? Was she really going on a date with Sandy King, The Net-breaker?

She pinched herself to make sure she wasn't dreaming.

Then her phone went. It was Wallace Drummond with news that brought her back to earth with a crash.

VIII

Ewan had taken details from Alice Rogerson at Aberstyle Farm. She had discovered the burglary herself two mornings previously when she came in from helping her husband with the morning milking. It had been a professional job, clinically performed.

'They must have known precisely when we were out of the house,' she told him. 'And they took my grandfather's collection of tobacco tins, including one that he had when he was in the trenches on the Somme. That was what hurt most. It was sentimental, you see.'

And apart from that they had taken all of her jewellery and her husband's Omega watch.

After that he had ridden across to Strathcombe, a hamlet of five crofts where three of them had been burgled the night before. And, as in the Rogerson case, they had been niftily done when the owners were all out tending to their crofts.

'Professionals are at work here,' Ewan mused as he pedalled into action. 'That strikes me that they are not local folk then. No one here on West Uist would have any idea about this burgling. I'll get the others interviewed then get back and see if I can't see some pattern that will lead me to the culprit.'

He glanced at his watch and decided the best route towards the next case, which was over on the west of the island.

'Och it will be best to go past Sharkey's Boot, I am thinking.' Then he remembered that Rab McNeish lived on Sharkey's Boot and he had been about to complain of a theft, until he had been scared away by Annie McConville.

'Torquil is always going on to me about taking initiative. Well, maybe this is just the sort of thing he meant. Maybe Rab McNeish would like me to investigate his theft. He said it was at his house. Antiques!'

He patted the moped's handlebars. 'Come on, Nippy, let's show that initiative. Sharkey's Boot it is and McNeish's half-complaint about burglary.'

He had only gone a quarter of a mile when his phone went and he had to stop to answer it.

It was Morag.

'Ewan, we need you back right away.'

'But Morag, I think — '

'And on your way, stop at the mortuary and get a bag from Dr McLelland. He's expecting you.'

'But Morag, do you — ?'

'Be quick, Ewan, there's a pet. Torquil wants me to meet him and the twins at Dr Dent's cottage, so I need you to look after the station.'

IX

Torquil tied Crusoe to the drain pipe then unlocked the front door with the key found among Dr Dent's possessions. He patted the dog then stood and turned to the others.

'Did Ralph say anything else when you phoned him?' he asked Morag.

'Just to take water specimens from this tank that the boys saw and any other possible places where he could have been drowned.'

'In that case, don't forget the garden pond there,' suggested Wallace.

Torquil pushed the door open and gingerly stepped inside, carefully examining the floor for any signs of anything unusual.

'There are scuff marks on the carpet,' he

pointed out. 'Take care as you come in, folks, and walk round them. Morag you'd better photograph them.'

'I have all the forensic gear with me, boss. I'll start taking shots as soon as you say so.'

Torquil nodded and went into the front room that had indeed been decked out as a laboratory. In an umbrella stand were a series of sticks, canes and the broken gossamer insect net that he himself remembered Dr Dent complaining about.

'Someone has been in here, right enough. They've been through his books,' said Torquil. Then he pointed towards a desk that was littered with papers, journals and print-outs. 'And it looks as if his paperwork has had a bit of a going through. The question is, was it before or after he was murdered?'

'I don't like the atmosphere in this room,' Douglas said with a shiver. 'It has an evil feel to it.'

'And it sounds as if there is running water somewhere,' added Wallace.

Torquil crossed to the tank and bent to take a closer look at it.

'Well, this is the sound of running water. There's a pump that is keeping water flowing. Look, there is one pipe coming in and presumably one flowing out. What on earth can this be here for?'

'Something to do with his midge studies?' Morag suggested.

'Maybe,' Torquil replied and followed the pipes out of a far door that led into a hall.

'Right enough,' he said a moment later. 'There is a pump here from the bath and back again. The bath is full. We'd better have specimens from both the bath and the tank, Morag. Make sure you label clearly which is which.'

'What do you think, boss?' Morag asked.

'I think this is something to do with his midge studies, right enough. Possibly he needed to simulate flowing water, like a river or stream.'

'Was he drowned here, do you think?' Douglas asked warily.

Torquil knelt and looked at the pool of water on the floor round the bottom of the tank. He rubbed his chin.

'It is certainly possible. The water is pretty near the top so if a body was held under the water it would displace it all over the floor.'

'But wouldn't it be everywhere?' Morag asked.

'It would if he struggled.'

'He was quite a big chap,' Morag pointed out. 'It would have taken a lot to overpower him.'

'It would if he was conscious and able to struggle.'

Douglas shivered. 'Ugh! That sounds horrible. Holding an unconscious man under the water.'

'That would be someone making no mistake about killing him then,' Wallace ventured.

'Aye, and that means that the scud on the head that he had could be more significant. He could have been knocked out and then drowned, before the murderer had a good skulk around.'

'So you are not thinking it was a case of a botched robbery,' Morag asked.

'No, I think we need to have a good look about for something that might have been used to knock him out. I am betting that we won't find it inside the cottage. You lads go and have a look outside. See if you can find anything that could have been used. It might have blood on it.'

When the twins had left Morag set about photographing the room as Torquil stood up, thinking.

'I am going to switch that pump off, Morag,' he said after a few moments.

'Why, is the noise bothering you?'

'No, it is just that if Dr Dent had been drowned in that tank, which I rather think he was, then there may well be blood cells floating about in it. And there might be some in the bath as well, since the pump is keeping up a flow. I may be grabbing at straws, but maybe Ralph could tell us if there are more in the tank than the bath.'

'What do you think the murderer was looking for among his books and papers?'

'I don't know, Morag. But I am guessing that we won't find very much, even after we have been through all of this. Which may take a long time, considering that a lot of it will probably be scientific jargon.'

'Why don't you think we'll find much?'

'Because I am more concerned about what isn't here.'

'I don't get you?'

'He is a scientist, yet there is no computer. There is a router on the desk, but where is his PC, or his laptop? I reckon that is what the murderer was looking for.'

There was a tap on the door and Wallace put his head round.

'Do you want to have a look here, Torquil? Douglas has just fished a stone gnome out of that pond.'

'A gnome?'

'Aye, a garden gnome, one of those that looks as if he's fishing. When we were crossing what was once the lawn we found the gnome's fishing net. Then we saw its face and hands peeking up through the water lilies.' He winced. 'I bet the murderer grabbed that then threw the fishing net aside. After it was done he lobbed it in the pond. There looks to be blood on the little devil's hands.'

'And a broken fishing net. Just like Dr Dent's,' said Torquil. 'There's irony.'

X

After six paracetamol Fergie had finally managed to gain some ease from the stabbing pains in his head that had felt as if someone had stirred up a hornet's nest. In its place he had been left with a bee in his bonnet. And this simply would not go.

The old bugger made a right mug of us, he thought to himself, as he drove towards Half Moon Cove. I'll get him to come on the show if I have to kidnap him to do it.

He grinned. Chrissie would not be pleased if she knew what was in his mind. Still, if I bring off this coup, I'm sure she will be . . . grateful.

He parked the Mercedes off the track among sand dunes so that it would not be spotted from the house, then he made his way around the tall perimeter fence.

Sod the front gate and that blooming intercom of his. He will hardly be able to turn me away when I have shown such initiative.

He scaled the fence and made his way across the undulating sand dunes towards the house. To his surprise he found the back door standing ajar.

'Anyone home?' he called out, as he pushed open the door and let himself in. 'Hello!'

But there was no answer.

He walked through a large clinically clean kitchen, then a hall, to enter a huge studio that looked outwards towards the sea. Lace curtains were draped across the large bay windows. In one of them a long telescope was set up and aimed seawards at a height that could be readily used from the high stool that stood behind it.

He wrinkled his nose at the all pervading smell of stale cigarettes.

'You like your whisky,' he said aloud, spying a side table with a half-empty bottle of Glen Corlan and an empty glass beside it.

Then his gaze took in the benches and tables of driftwood sculptures, many of them covered in dust, and dozens of packets and boxes.

You look like you are a busy bee sending stuff all over the place, even if you're not so busy sculpting these days. Hello, what's this for?

He crossed to the back of the studio where a large chest freezer hummed away like some weird futuristic sarcophagus.

I guess you have to be well-stocked up if you choose to live like a recluse.

Curiosity overcame him and he lifted the lid and looked inside.

His eyes gaped and a cry of alarm started to rise in his throat. But it died on his lips the moment a heavy piece of timber smashed into the back of his skull. His hairpiece flew off and hit the wall and was instantly spattered with blood.

9

I

Cora had not been keen on meeting Wee Hughie at the Bonnie Prince Charlie, but she reconciled it in her mind as being good investigative journalism experience.

Just as long as he doesn't suggest anything creepy, she thought as she walked along Harbour Street towards the bar.

I just don't know why he seemed so keen on meeting me? He's not my type with all those big muscles. Why should he think I would go for that?

She was still puzzling the question when she entered the lunchtime throng. A shrill whistle immediately rang out and she looked round, as did all of the other customers.

'Cora! Over here! I have got us a table,' Wee Hughie called, as he stood to tower over a group of men who had clearly just disembarked from one of the yachts in the harbour.

Cora suppressed the impulse to turn tail. Instead she brazened the looks of amusement and disdain as she sidled through the crowd towards him. It was clear that some people remembered her last visit to the Bonnie Prince Charlie, when she and Calum had been asked to leave.

Come on, Cora, she chided herself. You want to be a journalist, don't you? Just get used to being a pariah like Calum. And with that resolve she reached Wee Hughie and forced a smile.

'This is so good of you to come,' he said enthusiastically, his cheeks looking quite rosy.

'It's — er — good of you to ask me.'

He crinkled his nose in a manner that made her picture a goofy boxer dog. 'I just thought it would be — you know — nice.'

She let him relieve her of her jacket then sat while he went off to the bar to order drinks.

The large plasma screen TV was louder than she would have liked, considering the proximity of the table that Wee Hughie had obtained for them.

'I've got us a menu,' Wee Hughie said, a few moments later as he handed her a lemonade and lime. 'Do you like that soft drink stuff?' he asked, with a nod at her drink before taking a hefty swig of his pint of Heather Ale. He smacked his lips and licked the foam off his upper lip. 'You don't know what you're missing, Cora. We don't get anything like this in Dundee.'

'I'm afraid that I don't drink much alcohol, Mr — er — '

'Hughie! Just call me Hughie.'

Cora smiled. 'I like to be in control, you see. Alcohol does things to the mind.'

Wee Hughie winked at her and took another swig of beer. 'I'll drink to that any day.' Then seeing what he perceived to be disapproval on her face he added rapidly, 'But see, I hardly ever drink myself. It's only if I'm on a bit of a holiday like this.' He clapped his hands. 'So, what would you like to eat? A steak? The fisherman's pie? I hear that the seafood platter is good.'

Cora pursed her lips apologetically as she continued to scan the menu. 'I don't think there's much here for me — er — Hughie. You see, I'm vegetarian.'

'Really?' he asked, his eyes opening so wide that his eyebrows rose a full inch. Then he smiled and leaned forward on his elbows. 'You know, I've fancied being a veggie. Why don't you choose what you want and I'll have the same?'

Cora feigned delight and then looked over the menu again to see what was the most unappetizting meal available in the meagre list of vegetarian options. 'Well how about macaroni and cheese?'

Wee Hughie excused himself and went to

place their order at the bar. When he returned Cora asked him, 'So what can I do for you?'

'Oh, a lot, Cora,' he replied, with the slightest of leers.

Cora suppressed the urge to throw his beer into his lap. Ignoring his innuendo, she went on, 'What brings you to West Uist?'

'A sporting holiday. My boss, Dan Farquarson, loves his fishing and hunting.'

'And what about your friend, Mr King, was it?'

'He's a business friend of my boss, Cora. Nothing to do with me. But I have to say that the boy is good fun. He's a famous footballer, you know.'

Cora shook her head with a smile. 'I didn't know that. But he looks like a chap who likes a bit of fun.'

And she cringed as she said it lest Wee Hughie take this as an innuendo directed at him. In truth, she found the big man anything but fun. She quickly tried to deflect any response. 'Do you think — ?'

To her surprise he shushed her.

'Sorry Cora, it's the News. I am sort of expecting something. The boss told me to keep an eye on it for him.'

Cora nodded, sat back and listened to Kirstie Macroon's dulcet voice reading the headlines from an auto-cue with professional ease.

'We bring you the very latest news from West Uist.'

Cora's ears pricked up and she sat forward again.

'Inspector Torquil McKinnon of the West Uist Division of the Hebridean Constabulary has informed us this morning that there have been serious doubts cast over the sudden death of Dr Digby Dent, the noted entomologist who had been working on the island.'

'Bloody hell!' Cora muttered.

'Inspector McKinnon was unable to go into details but informed us that the police are treating the death as a case of suspected murder. We shall be bringing you more news as and when it becomes available to us.'

Cora felt her mouth suddenly go dry. She took a sip of her drink then turned to Wee Hughie.

'Listen, I'm afraid that I am going to have to cut and run. You see — '

Then she noticed how pale he had suddenly gone.

'Oh — er — of course,' he replied. 'I think I had better be getting back as well.

'Is anything wrong, Hughie?'

'Wrong? No, nothing's wrong, hen. I just — er — remembered something I need to pick up for the boss.' He glanced at his watch then raised his pint and drained it quickly. 'I'll settle up and then I'll shoot off. Maybe we could do this another time?' he asked with a smile.

'Yes, maybe,' Cora replied.

His forced smile had failed to convince her.

II

Calum had turned on the TV in the *Chronicle* offices while he waited for Sandy King to arrive for the agreed interview. He stood staring in disbelief as Kirstie Macroon read out the headlines. His mouth gaped wider and wider.

' . . . *We shall be bringing you more news as and when it becomes available to us.*'

'Unbelievable!' he howled at the TV. 'Torquil McKinnon, you rotten swine!' He stood staring at the mug in his hand for a moment and then dashed it against the wall where it shattered into a myriad of pieces and stained the wall, over an already aged and dried stain from a previous act of long-forgotten petulance.

'You traitor!' he yelled.

He only dimly heard the footsteps on the stairs behind him.

'I hope you are not talking about me?'

Calum spun round to find Sandy King standing at the top of the stairs. 'Oh, it's you.'

Sandy King raised an eyebrow. 'You seemed keener than that to get me here, Mr Steele. Is this a bad time?'

Calum recovered himself and leapt forward. 'Not at all! Not at all! And please, call me Calum. It's just that I've — er — had a spot of bad news.' He sucked air through his teeth and held his hands out, palms upward as if seeking understanding from the divine.

'I have been betrayed, Sandy.'

'Are you talking about the News? I caught the tail end of it as I was coming up. It was about Dr Dent, wasn't it? They think he's been murdered.'

Calum nodded and grimaced as if he was in pain. 'Aye, that's what's bothering me. He should have told me, not gone behind my back to Scottish TV.'

'Who?'

'Torquil McKinnon, the local inspector. He's supposed to be my friend and there he's gone and stabbed me in the back. There is no such thing as honour these days.'

Sandy King sat down on the settee and crossed his legs. 'I am not so sure, pal. I think it is still about. In fact, for some people, honour is the guiding principle in their life.'

III

Leaving Morag and the twins to complete the further investigation of Dr Dent's cottage, Torquil had put Crusoe in the side pannier of the Bullet then set off for home.

He found Lachlan and Kenneth Canfield coming along the road from the golf course.

'We were chased away today,' Lachlan said cheerfully as Torquil coasted to a halt beside them.

'Midges?' Torquil asked.

Kenneth Canfield laughed. 'And not even Lachlan's evil-smelling pipe could keep them off us.'

Lachlan ruffled the fur on Crusoe's head. 'You wouldn't have liked the golf course today, boy. Those midges would have invaded your fur and made mincemeat out of you.' He put his unlit pipe in his mouth and addressed his nephew. 'What are you doing home at this time of the day, anyway?'

'I came to have a word with you both actually. About Dr Dent.'

'Ah, the midge man,' said Kenneth. 'I was so sorry to hear about his accident.'

'It was no accident,' Torquil said bluntly.

'No accident?' Lachlan repeated.

'I believe it was murder, Uncle. We have started a murder investigation. Which is why I

233

wanted to have a word with the Reverend Canfield. I understand that you knew him from the University of the Highlands?'

Kenneth sighed. 'I wondered when you would get around to me, Inspector.'

'Shall we go into the manse and talk in comfort?' Lachlan suggested. 'It will soon be time for lunch.'

Five minutes later they were all seated in the spacious sitting-room. Crusoe was as usual curled up at Torquil's feet.

'How long had you known Dr Dent?' Torquil asked.

'About seven years. He was already in post when I became the university chaplain.'

'Did you like the man?'

'That's a direct question, Inspector. I suppose it deserves a direct answer. No! I did not like him and I did not respect him.'

'And the reason being?'

Canfield licked his lips and his eyes unconsciously fell on the whisky decanter.

'He had a reputation as a philanderer. I had been involved in two cases of students who had been hurt by him. Emotionally bruised, both of them.'

'Do you mean that he had relationships with them? I thought that was a sackable offence.'

'Potentially, it can be. Although in these

days . . . ' He shrugged. 'Yet in both cases the lassies did not want to make an issue of it.'

'So you disliked him because of his morals?'

'That and the fact that he was a maverick, academically speaking. Some of his research was regarded as questionable, although it has to be said that some folk thought he was brilliant.'

He glanced again at the decanter and this time Lachlan caught his look and acted upon it. He rose and poured two large drams then held the decanter up and eyed Torquil questioningly.

'None for me thanks, Lachlan,' Torquil said. Then, turning again to Kenneth, 'Is there anything else that you can tell me about Dr Dent that might help?'

Lachlan handed Kenneth his drink and then cleared his throat meaningfully. Kenneth understood his prompt.

'There might be something. Heather McQueen, the post graduate student who was drowned last summer. Well, she was his student. He was supposed to be looking after her.'

'Was he having an affair with her?'

Kenneth took a large gulp of whisky and then pursed his lips thoughtfully. 'I honestly don't know. But I suspect he was. At the very least I think that he should have shown more remorse than he did.'

'What do you mean?'

'She was his responsibility. He just didn't seem to acknowledge anything about it. In my book that makes him seem a bit of a psychopath.'

Lachlan ran a finger round the rim of his glass. 'I told Torquil about the grave, Kenneth.'

'Did you put flowers on her grave?' Torquil asked.

'No.'

'Any idea who did?'

'I think it could have been Digby Dent. But I suppose we'll never know now. It will remain a mystery.'

Torquil nodded and absently reached down and stroked Crusoe. He was rewarded by a lick on his hand.

Another mystery, he mused. Just like Crusoe here.

IV

Torquil had barely sat down in his office after lunch when the phone went and Morag told him that there was a call on the line.

'It's Calum Steele and he sounds peeved,' she said, unable to keep the mirth from her voice.

It was an understatement. 'You are a

traitor, Torquil McKinnon! How could you do that? You betrayed me — and to Kirstie Macroon. You know that I have feelings for her the same way that you do about Lorna.'

'Calum!'

'That makes me look a right fool. And I thought you were my friend.'

'Calum, listen.'

'That's all I ever do is listen. That's what journalism is all about.'

'In that case have you ever heard the expression about glass houses and throwing stones?'

'What are you on about?'

'If you live in a glass house you shouldn't throw stones.'

'Are you going daft? I am talking about loyalty and you betrayed me. You went to the Scottish TV with a story when you should have come to me. I won't forget this, Torquil.'

There was a click and Torquil found himself listening to the dialling tone.

'Well, you are welcome, Calum,' he said as he replaced the receiver. 'For someone with skin so thick, you are remarkably sensitive.'

But Calum's mention of Lorna's name rankled him. He sat patting Crusoe for a few moments then picked up the phone and dialled Lorna's mobile. She picked up after the third ring.

'Hello, it's the Scotch egg Carry-out here,' he joked. 'Any requests for lunch?'

Lorna laughed, then to his surprise said, 'Torquil, gosh, this is not a good time. The boss is on the warpath. Got to go. I'll ring you sometime. Don't ring me.'

Once again the phone went dead and he found himself listening to the dialling tone. He sighed and replaced the receiver again. 'No one loves me today,' he grumbled.

The sound of Crusoe's tail thumping the floor made him look down and feel better.

'Well, let's just hope that Lorna takes to you the way that you have taken to me, my lad. Now let's get cracking. We have a murder case to crack.'

V

Ewan was just about to go through to the kitchen to make tea for the meeting when the station door opened and the bell tinkled. He looked round then gaped. It was Chrissie from the *Flotsam & Jetsam* TV show and a gaunt, young-looking chap with longish hair.

'Ah, Officer,' said Chrissie. 'We've got a problem. I am Chrissie Ferguson from *Flotsam & Jetsam* and this is Geordie Innes, our producer.'

'It's a pleasure, Miss — er — ' Ewan began,

238

his cheeks starting to glow in the presence of the famous hostess of the TV show.

'We've lost Fergie Ferguson!' Geordie Innes stated bluntly. 'You need to find him.'

'You've lost him. A missing person, you say?'

Chrissie stared at him as if she thought he was simple-witted. 'My husband Fergie Ferguson. He's famous. Everybody knows him, so he shouldn't be hard to find on a wee island like this.'

'Have you looked for him?'

'Of course we've looked for him,' replied Geordie tartly. 'And we can't find him, which is why we've come to you.' He glanced irritably at his watch. 'We have a show in a few hours.'

'Ewan pulled his pencil from his pocket and opened up the day book. 'When did you last see him?'

'This morning.'

'Just this morning? He's not been gone very long then?'

'No, but he could be drinking,' Chrissie said. 'He sometimes does this when he's stressed. He goes on a bit of a bender.'

'I can't really help you then. We can't do anything until he's been missing for twenty-four hours.'

'But he has a show in a few hours!' Chrissie exclaimed.

'He could be lying in a ditch drunk as a lord,' said Geordie.

'If he's still not shown up by tomorrow, then come back and we'll look into it.'

Chrissie opened her mouth as if to say something then shook her head, turned round and flounced out.

'Have you tried all of the pubs?' Ewan suggested to Geordie.

'No, but if he doesn't show up soon I'm probably going to find a corner of one and stay there myself. Without Fergie Ferguson we're screwed!'

VI

Torquil looked round as Ewan came in with the tray laden with tea and biscuits.

'Any problem out there, Ewan?'

'Fergie Ferguson may have gone on a bender. That was Chrissie and their producer. He's gone off somewhere and they're worried about the show later.'

'They haven't left it very long,' said Morag. 'As if we haven't got enough on our hands already.'

'That's showbiz folk for you, though,' said Wallace.

'Demanding!' agreed Douglas.

'OK, folks; let's see where we have got to. Ewan first: have you anything to add on those thefts?'

'I've made reports, but I haven't finished seeing everyone.'

'OK, we'll look at them separately later. Morag, did you find anything from the University of the Highlands?'

'I talked to all sorts of folk, from the vice chancellor downwards. Jenny Protheroe, the head of the HR department told me that he had a reputation as a bit of a Lothario. She implied that he would have a go at anyone in a skirt, although she sounded peeved that he hadn't had a go at her. She also mentioned Heather McQueen, the girl who drowned last year. She was a postgraduate student of his.'

Torquil frowned. 'Yes, I talked with the Reverend Canfield, the chaplain at the university. He said that he thought Dent should have been more remorseful about her death. A cold fish, it seems.'

'Aye, a cold fish that swam in other folk's school of fish, it seems,' said Wallace.

'A bit of a shark,' said Douglas.

Torquil picked up the marker and added the name Heather McQueen to the board and drew a circle round it. Then he drew a line between her circle and Dr Dent's and added a question mark.

'The FAI didn't draw any conclusions about it,' Morag said.

'What do we know about her?' Torquil queried.

'Next to nothing,' Morag said. 'I'll get on to it. Shall I give Dr McLelland a ring and ask him if he can remember anything strange about her post-mortem?'

'Good idea,' Torquil said with a nod. 'You can ask him when you tell him about the other things we want him to check out. Now, about Dr Dent's cottage. We found a water tank and we need to have the water checked for Dr Dent's blood. We found signs of a burglary, although we think that was what the murderer wanted us to think. And it seems there is a missing computer.' He made notes under Dr Dent's name.

'And we found the likely murder weapon.'

Ewan shuddered and pointed to the concrete gnome with bloody hands that stood, bagged up in polythene on the table tennis table. 'Is that what was used?'

'It looks like it,' said Wallace.

'We found it in a garden pond.'

'All of which leaves the main question,' Torquil went on. 'Why was his body then dumped on the moor?'

VII

Morag arrived at Arbuckle's wine bar on Deuglie Street at ten past eight, having made sure that she was ten minutes late on purpose. She was as nervous as a sixteen year old meeting a boy on a first date. Her heart was pitter-pattering and she was sure that her cheeks were flushed.

Sandy King was sitting at a corner table sipping a glass of iced water. He sprang to his feet upon her entry and crossed the bar to meet her.

'Morag, thanks for coming,' he said, reaching down and giving her an air kiss. 'A nice wee place you chose here. Good atmosphere and the food smells fabulous.'

'It's as discrete as you can get on our wee island,' she returned, letting him pull out a chair for her.

'I can see that,' he replied with a grin. 'I already gave Rosie, the barmaid, my autograph.'

'You can't expect to keep your identity secret even on West Uist. Not when you are Scotland's best hope to rival Wayne Rooney.'

He averted his eyes with embarrassment. 'I wouldn't put myself in that class.'

'We can all hope.'

'Indeed. But my cover will be all blown

tomorrow. I gave Calum Steele of the *Chronicle* an interview today. Odd wee chap isn't he?'

'Calum is a one-off.'

'Aye you can say that again. He was a bit upset, actually. I came in when he was watching the news and he seemed put out over something to do with Dr Dent's death.'

'He felt my inspector should have told him and not the Scottish TV.'

'Ah! So that was it. Still, enough of all that. This evening is about you and me.'

Morag's cheeks started to burn and she looked down to see his hand reach out to touch hers.

And despite her nerves, she did not withdraw it.

VIII

Torquil had just come in from giving Crusoe an evening run. Lachlan was sitting on the floor in the hall working on the carburettor of the Excelsior Talisman motor cycle that they had both been slowly rebuilding for the past two years.

'Ralph McLelland rang while you were out, Torquil. He has to go out on a house visit over at Fintry Farm, but he'd like to meet you at the mortuary in half an hour. He says it is important.'

Lachlan wiped a grease trail across his forehead with the back of his wrist then sat tapping the carburettor with an expanding spanner. 'And just after he called, our old friend Superintendent Lumsden phoned to say that you are to call him straight away when you get in.' He clenched the spanner so that his knuckles went white. 'The man is so rude; I know what I'd like to do with this spanner.'

'Uncle, that's not a Christian thought.'

'I have already asked forgiveness for it, but that man would try a saint. Maybe you had better get him on the blower.'

Torquil went through and called his superior officer up on his mobile. 'Good evening, Superintendent Lumsden. You wanted me — '

'Why haven't I had a report through, McKinnon?'

'I am still at a preliminary stage of — '

'You know what I said, McKinnon. I want to be kept informed at every step. You think you can get away with anything over on that cursed island.'

'It is not a cursed island, Superintendent.'

'What progess have you made?'

'Slow progress, but I think we have established that it was definitely murder. His

245

head was bashed in with a concrete gnome.'

'A gnome!' The superintendent's voice fairly blasted down the phone. 'Are you serious?'

'We found it covered in blood in Dr Dent's garden pond.'

'But he was found on the moor?'

'I think the murderer moved his body.'

'Good grief! This gets worse! Get me a report on my desk by noon tomorrow.'

'Yes, Superintendent, but about Sergeant — '

The phone clicked and all he heard was the dialling tone.

'Thank you for your support as usual, Superintendent Lumsden,' he said wryly as he snapped the phone shut.

IX

The lights were on in the mortuary and Dr Ralph McLelland's battered old Bentley was parked in front of it as Torquil rode the Bullet into the cottage hospital car-park. He pressed the intercom button and spoke into it.

'Come away in, Torquil,' Ralph's vaguely distorted voice called back. 'I am in the lab.'

Torquil found him sitting by his micro-scope.

'Is it about the water samples, Ralph?'

'You were right; there is blood in the pond,

the water tank and the bath water. That makes it look as if he was drowned some time ago in the tank, then the water there and in the bath must have circulated for quite some time. And it looks as if the murder weapon was tossed into the pond.'

'Any idea how long he had been dead?'

'No. But that wasn't actually what I wanted to see you about: it was about that girl who drowned last year, Heather McQueen. You remember the other day that I said I had a bad feeling about all this?'

'Aye, I do. But I don't follow you.'

'It was about Dr Dent's body not being in the right place. Then when Morag Driscoll told me that you wanted to know if there was anything odd about Heather McQueen's post-mortem, it suddenly struck me.' He pointed to the microscope. 'I looked out the tissue specimens I took at her post-mortem and the water samples that I collected from her lungs.'

'She was drowned in Loch Hynish. Surely that's all that there was to it.'

'Oh she was drowned all right. But Loch Hynish is a freshwater loch.'

'You have me worried now, Ralph. What is it?'

'She had sea water in her lungs. I didn't do the test at the time, it didn't seem necessary.

But now that I have it is clear — she drowned in the sea.'

'Are you serious? That means we have two bodies that were drowned.'

Ralph nodded and clicked his tongue. 'And for some reason, maybe for different reasons, both bodies were moved.'

Torquil thumped the bench so that the microscope shook.

'Damn it! And that makes it likely that we have two murders here, not just the one!'

10

I

Morag found it hard not to walk around with a smile on her face the next morning. Ewan noticed it straight away, but was polite enough to wait until he had made her a mug of tea before asking her.

'Did you have a good evening, Sergeant Morag?'

'It was bliss, Ewan. Sandy is so . . . nice!'

'Are you seeing him again?'

'Uh huh. Tonight. We have — '

The door banged open and the Drummond twins came in. They were not so reticent.

'You look flushed, Morag Driscoll. You must have had a good time with that football lad,' said Douglas.

'You just remember that you have wee ones at home. Not too much gallivanting at nights now,' added Wallace.

'I . . . I . . . don't know what you — '

'Yes you do,' interrupted Wallace with a wink.

And before she could reply to this the door

opened again and Torquil bounced in with Crusoe at his heels. He had his Cromwell helmet in one hand and a dossier of notes in the other. 'I'll be needing to get an extra helmet soon,' he said, grinning at the dog.

Morag coughed. 'Yes, well, I had been meaning to have a word with you about that, Torquil McKinnon. It is not legal to be riding about on that motor cycle with a dog in your pannier.'

Torquil stared at her for a moment, then noticed the amused, knowing looks on the faces of the others. He grinned, then asked, 'Did you have a good evening, Morag?'

And then even before she could reply, he suddenly turned serious and waved the dossier in the air. 'Come on, everybody into the rest room. There have been more developments. Ralph called me in last night to the mortuary. We have two murders on our hands now.'

To their amazement he told them of Ralph's findings about Heather McQueen.

'So, Morag, we really do need as much information about her as possible.'

'I had it as my first task today already,' she replied.

'And, Ewan, I want you to go over and have a word with Rab McNeish.'

'Why is that, Torquil? Is that so-called

burglary of his relevant to these deaths?'

'What so-called burglary, Ewan?' Torquil asked.

'Oh, didn't I report it? Well it was weird actually. He came in to complain, like he always did. Then he said he had been sort of robbed, or something like that. Then Annie McConville came in and gave him what-for about his complaint about her. He got flustered then said he didn't want to make a report and left.'

'And so you didn't record it as a burglary after all?'

'Well, no. He retracted the whole thing.'

Torquil stood frowning. 'Maybe all the more reason to have a word, then.'

'And — er — what am I asking him about? I mean, is it just about this burglary?' He scratched his head. 'Because I am confused, sir. If it isn't about that, then why am I going?'

'Because he's an undertaker, Ewan,' Torquil replied, adding the name to the board and adding a circle to it. He drew a line between his circle and that of Heather McQueen. 'He did her funeral.'

He tapped the end of the marker on the board as he looked at the notes he had made in the dossier that lay before him 'And then there was another little puzzle that adds to this whole mystery.' He wrote the word flowers under Heather McQueen's circled name. 'Lachlan found that someone had put flowers on her grave the other day. I asked the Reverend Canfield about it and he thinks they were put there by Digby Dent.'

The bell rang out to alert them that someone had just entered the office. Ewan excused himself and went through to see.

It was a very agitated-looking Chrissie Ferguson and an equally anxious looking Geordie Innes.

'He hasn't come home all night,' Chrissie blurted out. 'Something's wrong!' she cried. 'You need to do something!'

'We had to cancel the show at the last minute, last night,' Geordie Innes said. 'Do you have any idea what that does to a show's ratings?'

'Bugger the ratings, Geordie!' exclaimed Chrissie in exasperation. 'Something is wrong, very wrong. This isn't just one of Fergie's benders. He always contacts me, even when he's ratted. Something is not right, I tell you. He had a bee in his bonnet about that old beachcomber refusing to come on the show after that Dent fiasco.'

Ewan calmly took all their details and their phone numbers and promised that they would start looking for him straight away and check with them about any progress later that morning.

Torquil was just about tying matters up when he returned to the rest room. Ewan gave him a quick report about Fergie Ferguson.

'She said he had a bee in his bonnet about Guthrie Lovat not coming on their show.'

Torquil tapped the name *Flotsam & Jetsam* on the board and the names of the presenters underneath. 'That is interesting. And he was peeved at Dr Dent, wasn't he? And now his wife says that Guthrie Lovat refused to come on their show after Dr Dent's death.'

'I remember that they were sort of gloating in anticipation on the night of the show when Dr Dent came on drunk. It sounds as if old Guthrie must have cried off.'

'What do you want us to do, Torquil?' Wallace asked.

'I want you to go to St Ninian's Cave and scour the beach. Crusoe was washed up on the beach. It is just an idea, but have a look to see what else washes up there. Maybe have a look at some other beaches about there.'

He looked at everyone. 'OK, are things clear? Let's reconvene at lunchtime.'

II

Twenty minutes later Torquil was sitting at his desk staring down at the cord and the strange knots that had been used to lash Crusoe to the timber. There was something about them that he couldn't seem to fathom.

His mobile went off and Lachlan's name flashed on the little screen.

'Torquil, I am with Kenneth Canfield. He has remembered something and he wondered if he ought to tell you.'

'Put him on, Lachlan.'

'Inspector McKinnon, I am sorry, but this has been niggling me. I know that I should have told you before. It is about Dr Dent and me.'

'I am listening.'

'I went to see him that afternoon. The afternoon before he went on the *Flotsam & Jetsam* show. I had gone to confront him about Heather McQueen. Well, we drank whisky. A lot of whisky.'

'That would account for him being so drunk on the TV show. And what about this discussion? What did you talk about?'

'That's just it, Inspector. I cannot remember anything about it.'

'Nothing?'

'Nothing, until I woke up in my hotel, vomiting my insides out. I had the hell of a headache.'

'Is that unusual for you?'

There was a guilty silence for a few

moments. 'I have a problem with whisky, Inspector, but I can usually hold a lot without any problem. I am so sorry that I didn't tell you before. I just felt so guilty and a bit frightened.'

'Thank you for this information, Reverend. You do realize that it makes you a suspect in his death?'

Again there was a pause. Then, 'Yes.'

'Right, I will need to talk to you in more detail later. Don't even think of trying to leave the island. I have already taken measures to stop all ferries from Kyleshiffin.'

Torquil sat for a moment after pocketing his mobile. Then he got up and grabbed his helmet. 'Come on, Crusoe, we're going to go for a ride.'

Morag was deep in conversation on the front phone when he went through.

'I am going off to Half Moon Cove,' he said softly.

'Why?' Morag mouthed.

'It is all to do with bees. Ewan said that Fergie Ferguson had a bee in his bonnet about Guthrie Lovat. Well I have a bee in my own bonnet that I can't get rid of. Maybe it will lead me to a hive. See you later.'

Morag waved then shook her head once the door had closed behind him. She had no idea what he was talking about.

III

Cora had come to work early and found that Calum had once again spent the night on his camp-bed. But to her relief she found that on this occasion there was no odour of stale whisky on his breath. Instead, he seemed to have a sparkle in his eye.

'I have been having a good think, Cora. I find that I think best in the *Chronicle* offices. Being close to all the stories that I have written over the years seems to energize me.'

Cora giggled. 'It sounds a bit mystical to me.'

'Aye, well, journalism is a bit like a mystical journey, Cora. There is nothing like it when you get a story between your teeth.'

She sat down beside him. 'I think I'm starting to get that feeling, boss.'

'Hey, let's drop the boss bit, shall we? It's just plain Calum.'

She beamed at him. 'I think your sixth sense might be starting to rub off on me. I sort of think I might have the essence of a story.'

'Excellent! Go on, lassie. Spring it on me.'

'Well, I think I know — I mean I think that maybe — Sandy King is here with Dan Farquarson because Farquarson is trying to buy him. You know, nobble him. Get him to throw matches and that. I was reading up about match-fixing on the internet. It is big business. Wee Hughie is Farquarson's muscle.'

Calum suddenly threw his arms about her and kissed her hard on the cheek. 'That's it! That's it! You've got the sense.'

He released her and they both beamed at each other. Then their proximity dawned on them.

'Oh!' said Cora.

'Ah!' said Calum.

'So . . . so what do we do now — er — Calum?'

'About what, Cora?'

'A-About Sandy King and Farquarson?' She averted her eyes and looked down at her feet. 'Or about us?' she whispered.

Calum swallowed hard. 'I think we need to have a drink, Cora.'

She nodded absently. 'You would like a whisky? Shall I get it?'

He patted the back of her hand affection-ately. 'No whisky, Cora. We have a story to chase. We need a cup of tea and some brain food. A mutton pie would be good.' He winked at her. 'Keep it professional, that's what I say. At least while we have a story to close down.' He smiled at her. 'And then we can talk about us.'

She brightened and gave him a peck on the cheek. 'Afterwards it is, Calum.'

IV

Ewan coaxed Nippy along the road towards Sharkey's Boot. It was hot and muggy and the midges were out in great swarms ready to ambush the unwary traveller. Considering the machine's age, the speedometer needle never came within five miles of its maximum thirty miles per hour, which made him an ideal target for the swarms.

'Blasted midges!' he exclaimed, swiping at them with one hand and swerving about the road as a result. 'I wonder if Dr Dent was getting closer to finding a solution for these wee nuisances?'

As he rode further into the huge haze of biting insects he scratched his neck, aware that already he had developed multiple tell-tale wounds. 'I can see why somebody could get obsessed with the wee scunners. They must spread all kinds of disease.'

And, as he said it, he thought of Rab McNeish, who certainly seemed to have some sort of phobia about dogs. 'Hmm! He sounded a bit subdued when I phoned him from the station. He didn't even swear once, which isn't like him. Still, we'll soon see. And it will be interesting to hear if he has anything to add about this Heather McQueen case. All a bit of a mystery.'

He cleared the swarm and heaved a sigh of relief. He was tempted to stop for a moment to pull up his collar to protect his neck as best he could against further midge attacks, but he did not want Nippy to lose speed, especially as there was a slight rise to negotiate before the road dropped down to the peninsula-shaped spit of land whose shape had given its name to Sharkey's Boot.

Towards the top of the rise he heard the noise of a vehicle coming in the other direction at speed. Then suddenly a canary yellow camper-van shot over the crest and zoomed towards him.

'You fools!' he yelled, as he swerved to avoid it.

He looked round immediately and saw it speeding off without stopping.

'Huh! It is those bird-watching lads again. I will be having words with them if I catch hold of them again. I already told them about speeding on West Uist.'

Then he cursed as Nippy's engine spluttered and threatened to stall. He began pedalling as hard as he could towards the crest of the rise.

V

Torquil opened up the throttle and let the Bullet have its head, conscious of Crusoe in the pannier.

'Ha! You actually like that, don't you, boy?' he yelled into the wind and was answered by a bark of pleasure. 'Now hold on, the road's a bit like a chicane for half a mile.'

And so saying he entered the series of snake bends that characterized the stretch of road as he headed towards Half Moon Cove.

He slowed as he saw Alec Anderson's mobile shop-cum Royal Mail van coming towards him.

He was about to wave as they approached one another but suddenly the haze of a midge cloud rose from the side of the road and, uncharacteristically, he faltered and the machine wobbled. It was all that he could do to maintain his balance.

The emporium van passed and once he had passed through the swarm he looked round at the retreating van. Then a couple of bars of a hornpipe rang out as the van horn was pumped.

Torquil grinned. 'Those blasted midges, Crusoe. That would be an inglorious end for us, ending up under the wheels of Alec Anderson's van.'

Crusoe barked, then whimpered and

started biting at his fur.

'Have you taken a few stray midges on board?' Torquil asked. 'Don't worry, I'll give the Bullet a burst on the next straight bit. That'll soon get rid of them.'

And with that he let the machine fly, much to Crusoe's pleasure and bark of obvious relief.

VI

Morag put the phone down and felt the blood drain from her cheeks. She was not sure that she could believe what she had just heard.

'It is not possible! I'd better tell Torquil.'

But before she did that she felt a hollow feeling expand within her and she felt the need, a desperate need, to talk to Sandy.

She phoned his mobile and waited. The phone was picked up after several rings and she heard his voice.

'Sandy, thank goodness. Listen I — '

' . . . in a moment you will be connected to the voice mail of — '

With a grunt of exasperation she pressed the cancel button.

'Why didn't you tell me this?' she moaned. She was about to phone Torquil then thought better of it.

'Damn! I wish one of the others was here.' She glanced at her watch and considered calling Ewan or the twins and bringing them back to look after the station. Then she made her decision. She locked up, grabbed the station's Escort car keys and let herself out of the back door.

VII

Calum and Cora had arrived at the luxury rented cottage on Calum's old yellow Lambretta. Calum had grinned all the way there at the warm feeling that having Cora's arms about his middle had given him.

You are a fool, Calum Steele; part of his mind had castigated himself. But she's a bonny lassie and she's lovely, another part protested.

And just to make him grin even more, from time to time he felt the grip tighten and he felt her face pressing against his back.

Be professional, Calum you numbskull! Later, you can ask her out.

He felt himself bristle when he turned off the engine and Wee Hughie appeared at the door. He came across the gravel to meet them, smiling broadly at Cora and ignoring him.

'I'm glad that you rang us, Cora,' Wee Hughie said. 'I wasn't sure what we were planning to do today. There's been a bit of a problem here.'

'What sort of problem?' Calum interjected, as he pulled off his helmet.

'A bit of a bust up between the boss and McNab. The bloke doesn't seem to know which side his bread is buttered.'

'What do you mean? Has Bruce McNab been dismissed?'

'He sacked us, more like,' returned Wee Hughie with a grin. 'The boss is fair annoyed. People don't talk to him like that.'

Cora smiled at Wee Hughie and Calum noticed how the big man melted. He could understand exactly how he felt, but it peeved him nonetheless.

'Could we come in and talk to Mr Farquarson?' Cora asked.

Wee Hughie laughed. 'And here was me thinking that you had come to talk to me! Of course you can. And then maybe later you and I could — '

'Actually, I think that Cora is going to be busy all day after we finish here,' Calum said quickly.

Wee Hughie glared at him. 'You'd better follow me then.'

And they followed him into the cottage and

263

found Dan Farquarson busily texting some-one on a Blackberry.

'Dan,' said Calum, ingratiatingly. 'Thanks for letting us have a few minutes.' He looked about the room. 'Er — where's Sandy?'

'I thought you wanted to speak to me, not Sandy,' Dan Farquarson asked without looking up from his Blackberry.

'Oh aye, it's you, Dan. For a feature in the *Chronicle*.'

'No feature!'

'Sorry?' Calum returned.

'I said, no feature. You can ask a few questions, but here are the rules first.' He pressed the send button on his phone then flicked it closed and looked up. 'You are the editor of the local rag, right? I am a Dundee businessman. I am here with my associate and with my good friend Sandy King. Those are facts. The first rule is you don't leap to any conclusions. We are here on a hunting holiday, not on any kind of business trip.'

'Of course, Dan,' Calum began. 'I wasn't suggesting that — '

Dan Farquarson smiled; a smile without any warmth whatsoever. 'Of course you weren't. You have already had an interview with Sandy King. The second rule is that there must be no adverse publicity. Nothing! Understand?'

Calum nodded emphatically. 'Totally understand, Dan. I just wanted — '

'You just wanted to stick your nose in and make some sort of connection, didn't you? You and your girlie here.' He nodded at Wee Hughie. 'Show him what we do to nosyparkers, Hughie.'

Wee Hughie stared at his boss and then at Calum. Then at Cora. With a shrug he stood up and took a pace towards Calum.

'Just you sit down, Hughie!' said Cora, shooting to her feet. 'What do you think you are doing listening to a windbag like that? He's just a big bully and he's using you, can't you see that?'

'Sit down, girlie!' Dan Farquarson snapped.

'Oh shut up, fatso,' Cora returned. 'We are not frightened of you. We are journalists. Calum Steele is the finest local paper editor in Scotland and he's not frightened of you and your big bank roll, wherever it came from.' She looked at Calum for support. 'You're not scared of the likes of him, are you, Calum?'

Calum stood and drew himself up to his full five foot six inches and puffed out his chest. 'Not a bit of it, Cora. And this little conversation has just confirmed all that we needed to know. Read the paper tomorrow, Farquarson, and sue me if you dare.'

'Hughie!' Farquarson screeched. 'Don't just stand there.'

But Wee Hughie just looked at his boss and despite himself he tossed back his head and roared with laughter. 'She's right. You are just a windbag. And you've even been sacked by your gillie today. Well, let me make it three. I've sacked you, too. You can find someone else to do your dirty work. I'm going off with my friends here. They can have all the information they want.'

The Dundee businessman huffed and puffed and then slumped down in his chair.

Wee Hughie walked outside with them.

'Cora, you are fantastic!' he said.

Cora started to tremble and Calum immediately put a protective arm about her shoulder before Wee Hughie could act. 'Aye, you were. And I am proud of you, lass. Dead proud.'

Wee Hughie shrugged as he saw the loving look she bestowed on Calum.

'Do you want me to follow you into town for a wee chat about Farquarson? I've been meaning to kick the old fart into touch for a while now. It's not the sort of work my old mother would like to see me doing.'

The sound of a car crunching up the gravel made them all turn. The West Uist police force's Ford Escort pulled up beside them and Morag Driscoll leaned out of the window.

'I need to speak to Sandy King,' she said, addressing all three of them.

'He's not here,' Wee Hughie volunteered. 'I'm not sure where he is, but I wouldn't be surprised if he had gone to sort things out with Bruce McNab.'

'That's what I'm worried about,' muttered Morag. 'Thanks,' she called, shoving the car into reverse and speeding back up the gravel drive.

VIII

Bruce McNab sat in his kitchen staring out of the window with a bottle by his side and his shotgun cradled over his knees. He had been drinking since cock crow. It was not something he normally did, but his spirits had sunk pretty low over the past few days. Farquarson's party had been an increasing irritation, what with them showing up as and when it suited them rather than as arranged. After his second drink he had phoned Farquarson and told him what he could do with his party!

But it had been the break-in that had really got to him. It had been made to look like a common burglary, but he knew better. Whoever had done it was looking for something — and they had found it. It had made him doubt his sanity for a while, since he was sure that he had hidden it away where no one could find it. It had been taken right enough, even though he had checked over his whole cottage at least six times, just in case he had moved it in a drunken haze one night.

He stared at the whisky glass in his hand, hesitating to drink it. Then he bent his head back and poured it down his throat, wincing as the liquid fire hit his stomach.

'You are a fool, McNab,' he growled at himself. 'Just like you were last summer. And now some bastard is coming for you.'

Out in their kennels his two chocolate Labradors started to bark.

'So you are about, are you? Well, come on, you bastard. If you want me, here I am!'

He ran a finger along the barrel of the gun and his face broke into a cynical sneer.

A trained hunter, he was normally aware of the slightest noise, but the whisky had dulled his senses. He hadn't heard the step behind him; hadn't even considered the possibility of someone getting into his house from the other side.

A hand shot over his shoulder and grabbed the shotgun.

'What the — ?' he began, as he tried to turn.

He yelled as the butt of the shotgun fell with great force on his right shoulder.

'Don't get up on my account, Bruce,' said Sandy King, walking round his chair into view. He was dressed in a black track suit and trainers. 'You were expecting me, I see. How nice.' He smiled as he broke the shotgun open and removed the cartridges. 'Let's just get rid of these. We wouldn't want anyone to get hurt, would we?'

Then the smile vanished as he pocketed the cartridges. 'I think it is time that we had a chat, don't you?'

11

Ewan had been relieved that he didn't have to run the gauntlet of any more midges on the road along Sharkey's Boot towards the row of crofts and outhouses where Rab McNeish lived and did the bulk of his carpentry and built his coffins.

He dismounted and stretched, then rubbed his neck where he seemed to have been bitten by hundreds of midges.

'Let's see if we can learn anything here then,' he said to himself, as he crunched over the gravel to the front door. He noted the repair work that had been done.

'I think his door must have taken a kicking,' he said. 'And it looks as if he has mended it himself. It is a great skill he must have with the hammer.' And he grinned to himself as he compared it to his skill with the Highland hammer.

He knocked on the door and stood waiting for a moment, fully expecting Rab McNeish to throw it open any moment. But there was no answer.

'Strange, he knew I was on my way,' he mused, as he knocked again.

Then he tried the door and found that it opened straight away into a neat and ordered little hall, with closed doors to the right and left.

'Mr McNeish? It's me, PC Ewan McPhee. Hello.'

There was no reply. He tapped on each door before opening them and popping his head round.

'What the dickens?' he said, as he stopped and strained his ears. 'Is that someone crying, I am hearing?' Then he shook his head. 'And now it sounds like an animal whining. More than one maybe.' And following the sound he retraced his steps outside and went round the back of the cottages to a row of outhouses. By the timber stacked up against the walls and the sawdust that covered the ground outside it looked as if these were Rab McNeish's workshops.

The noises were definitely getting louder.

He pushed open a door and stared in dis-belief. There were about a dozen cages each with a cowering ill-kept dog whimpering and shivering away. They seemed like mongrels mostly and most of them were skinny with corrugated rib cages showing.

'Goodness me! What's going on here?' he asked.

Then he saw the long bench with saws, various hunks of wood and something that looked like a cattle-prod lying on a bench.

The crying noise started again. A definite sobbing from behind the door. He took a step in and looked round.

Rab McNeish was curled up on the stone floor, almost in a foetal position, crying like a baby.

'F-Forgive me!' he moaned between sobs. 'It's the germs! The germs! They're going to kill me. They'll kill us all!'

Ewan felt a wave of nausea come over him. Rab McNeish was clearly in need of help that he couldn't give him. He pulled out his mobile and called Dr Ralph McLelland.

II

Morag drove up to Bruce McNab's cottage and quickly got out of the Escort. His dogs were barking furiously in their cages and she guessed that they had been barking away for some time, since by their eyes they seemed to be both distressed and angry. They were hurling themselves at the fronts of the cages in attempts to get out.

She didn't wait, but went straight for the door that stood ajar.

And then she heard Sandy's raised voice, cursing. And there was the sound of splashing water.

'Police!' she called, as she ran through the kitchen, noting the broken-open shotgun.

'Bastard! Is this how you did it?' she heard Sandy shout.

Along the hall she ran and burst into the bathroom.

Sandy King was staring wild-eyed, as he pushed Bruce McNab's bloodied face and head into the overflowing bath.

Morag stared in disbelief for a moment as she took in the scene. Bruce McNab was flailing about, but was being easily overpowered by Sandy. He held his head under the water and bubbles were streaming upwards.

'Sandy, for God's sake! You'll kill him!' she cried, dashing forward and grabbing his hands.

Sandy stared at her and snarled angrily. 'Back off!' Then he swung an elbow at her viciously and caught her on the side of the head. She tumbled sidewards and struck her head on the sink.

She slumped to the floor.

III

Torquil rode up the old track towards Half Moon Cove. The sand had been compacted by numerous tyre marks, leaving two continuous ruts with machair plants growing between.

'Hello? What's this?' he wondered, as a set of tracks suddenly left the track and disappeared into sand dunes.

He stopped the Bullet and pulled up his goggles to see better. 'Looks like a car went in but hasn't come out again.' He set off and turned into the dunes and found a Mercedes parked on its own. A fine patina of sand had already settled over the windscreen and bodywork.

'Looks as if it has been here a while, Crusoe,' he said to the dog in the pannier. 'Registration FNJ 1. I am thinking that has to stand for *Flotsam and Jetsam*. So it looks as if Mr Fergie Ferguson has been paying a visit on old Guthrie.'

He switched off the engine and dismounted. 'Come on then, Crusoe, we'll take a look.' He was about to set off when he noticed the footprints leading from the car. 'Curious and curiouser. Let's follow our TV man, since it looks as if he didn't go up the main track.'

And sure enough, although the winds from the sea had almost covered the prints, there was enough for Torquil to see that he had taken a circuitous route around the high fenced enclosure.

'Looks like he climbed over here, Crusoe. Which means I am going this way too.' He held out a stern hand. 'I want you to stay put. No noise. I won't be long.'

Crusoe whimpered, wagged his tail a couple of times, then settled down on his haunches and laid his head on the ground.

Torquil grinned then started shinning over the fence. He landed on the other side beside a couple of indentations where Fergie Ferguson seemed to have landed. Then he followed the tracks across more dunes until they came to the back door of the beachcomber's sprawling house.

He tried the door handle and it opened straight away.

'Hello! It is Inspector McKinnon of the West Uist Police.'

There was no answer.

'Mr Lovat? Mr Ferguson? Anyone at home?'

He made his way through a pristine clean kitchen, across a spartanly furnished hallway and into a long front room overlooking the sea. It was set out like a studio, with all sorts of driftwood, sculptures and piles of packets and boxes on benches.

'Anyone at home?'

He noted the telescope set up in the bay window with a bottle of Glen Corlan whisky nearby it. He picked it up and noted the sticker from Anderson's Emporium.

'I am guessing that Alec Anderson is about the only person to visit here,' he muttered.

Then he started to feel uneasy. There was

a chill in the room, despite the sun. And a noise.

He turned, localizing the noise to a huge chest freezer that was humming by a back wall.

'What's this for? Don't tell me old Guthrie is an ice-cream fanatic.'

He crossed to the freezer and idly lifted the lid.

The first thing he saw was what seemed like a bloody rat. Then he realized that it was a bloodstained hair-piece. But under it was a face with unseeing eyes staring up at him. Then he realized that he was looking at a dead body. Yet there were too many hands.

'My God! Two bodies!' he gasped.

'That's right, Inspector,' a voice snapped behind him. And then he felt something cold and hard dig into his back. 'This is a Glock semi-automatic. It's just over your spine and it will cut you in half if you so much as move a muscle. There is room in this freezer for a third body.'

IV

Dr Ralph McLelland had fortuitously been visiting a patient on the nearby Wee Kingdom. He answered Ewan's distress call straight away and quickly took charge.

276

'The poor chap is away with the fairies. I'll need to admit him to the cottage hospital under the Mental Health Act and then I'll need to get a psychiatrist over from the mainland. Meanwhile, you'll have to get the Scottish Society for the Prevention of Cruelty to Animals to come and take a look at these poor creatures. It looks as if he's been systematically abusing them.' He sucked air between his teeth. 'It's a bad business, Ewan. I reckon it will take time for them to come across, what with the restrictions on the ferries with the murder case. You might be as well just having a word with Annie McConville.'

'Aye, it is a pity that she doesn't like mobile phones. I could have given her a ring straight away.'

'Well, why don't you go and see her now? I will have to wait until Sister Lamb can get here to help me from the cottage hospital.'

Somewhat relieved to be able to leave the harrowing scene Ewan headed off on Nippy and was soon back on one of the side roads leading to Kyleshiffin.

As he turned on to the main road a familiar canary yellow camper-van came hurtling towards him. The driver peeped its horn at him and made to swerve round him, but Ewan held up his hand for it to stop.

Deliberately he dismounted, switched off

the engine and set the moped on its stand.

'What's wrong, Constable?' the swarthy driver asked, rolling down his window. The sun glinted off his ear-ring.

'Step out of the van would you?' Ewan asked. 'Both of you.'

With a huff of impatience the driver opened the door and got out. 'What's this about? We haven't got much time,' he demanded.

'I can see that. You two always seem to be in a hurry. Too much of a hurry. There have now been three occasions when I have been concerned abut the way that you handle this vehicle.'

'We're sorry, Officer,' said the slimmer and younger of the two. 'We'll be more careful.'

'Oh to hell with this lummox,' said the other. 'He can't do anything. We weren't breaking the law.'

'I do not like your tone, my man,' said Ewan.

'No? Well you'll just have to lump it, mate, because we're too busy to stop and chew the cud with the likes of you. Come on Tosh, let's get going.'

'Just a minute now,' said Ewan, grabbing hold of the man's arm.

In a trice the man darted a hand inside his camouflage jacket and drew out a gun.

'Christ, Craig, what are you playing at?'

exclaimed the lean one.

But Ewan had reacted instantly. He had grabbed them both around the neck at the same time bringing his knee up sharply to dash the gun from the one called Craig's hand. Then he bashed their heads together and held them until he felt them both slump into unconsciousness.

'I will not tolerate disrespect to the law,' Ewan said. 'And firearms are just as illegal here as on the mainland.'

He nudged the firearm away with his foot then reached down and handcuffed the two men together.

'Now let us see what you have inside this van of yours,' he said, walking to the rear and opening the door. He looked inside and stood gaping for a moment.

The noise of an approaching vehicle made him turn and he looked round to see the Drummond twins approach in their truck.

'Well, well, well, what have we here?' Wallace asked, as he climbed out.

'I have apprehended a couple of villains. It looks like they are the ones responsible for the spate of burglaries on the island.'

'And it looks as if they might be out of it for a while,' Douglas said with glee. 'They didn't know what they were doing when they picked on Ewan McPhee. Well done, big fellow.'

Ewan grinned proudly and bent down to retrieve the gun. 'Aye, a right pair of scunners these two. I don't know what Torquil will say when he hears that gun crime has come to West Uist.'

V

Morag felt water splashing on her face and hands on her shoulders.

The memory of Sandy King holding Bruce McNab's head under the water in the bath brought her back to sudden consciousness. She opened her eyes and saw Sandy King staring at her with wide open eyes.

She lashed out and caught him on the side of the head.

'Morag! You're OK! Thank the Lord.'

She clenched a fist to punch again, but stopped when she saw the concern on his face and she realized that the water had been splashed in her face to try and rouse her from unconsciousness, not an attempt to drown her.

'Sandy, what have you done — ?'

'To McNab? Just taught him a lesson. He'll be OK. Look.'

And she saw Bruce McNab was lying slumped against the bath. He was bleary-eyed and breathing heavily, but he was alive.

'We had a fight,' Sandy explained as she managed to sit up. 'Or rather, he fought a bit as I dragged him to the bath. If you hadn't come I might have taken it a bit further. But he deserves it, the useless piece of shit.'

'Heather McQueen was your sister, wasn't she?' Morag asked.

Sandy stood up and swallowed hard, his eyes filling up with tears. 'She was my half-sister. That's why we had different names. There were just the two of us left after my mum died. We were like chalk and cheese. She was bright and liked lads, while I was sporty and a bit over-focused on being a football star. We had a huge row on the phone one time, what about God only knows, but from then we didn't communicate, not even Christmas or birthday cards. Effectively we wrote each other out of our lives.

'Then I was off at soccer camps and then playing for one club or another. I was playing in Munich when it happened and I never found out until a month after. How do you think that felt? I was loaded with guilt.'

His eyes narrowed. 'How did you find out?'

'I went right back to basics and traced her birth, then — I found your name.'

'I studied everything about her death and just couldn't believe it. She was a great swimmer. I thought there had to be some man involved in all this. That was what Heather was about. And it all pointed to that Dent character. I found out that he was still working here on West Uist. When Dan Farquarson started making advances to me, I guess you'll find out about that, he wanted to get me in his pocket so that I could fix a match here or two. Well, it was the ideal opportunity to come here, so I persuaded him to arrange it.'

'And so you came to West Uist, for what? To get even?'

'To find out if he was responsible for her death. I was going to beat the hell out of him. And then I found out it wasn't him. It was this specimen!'

Bruce McNab's head had slumped on to his chest.

'But I'm getting ahead of myself. I found out where she was buried after I burgled the local newspaper office. Fancy that, eh? Me a common burglar! But I needed to look through the papers without anyone suspecting what I was doing. And when I went to lay flowers on her grave, low and behold, who did I find doing the same thing, but Bruce McNab.'

At the mention of his name Bruce McNab looked up. 'I deserved everything you gave me, King,' he said through puffed lips. 'Except I didn't do anything to your sister. I loved her, you know. I really loved her. We had an affair, a lovely, special affair. But she had to keep it all secret because of Digby bloody Dent. Why, I don't know.

'But that night we went out in the boat and got drunk. Doped up and drunk. I passed out and found her gone. I just assumed she had gone for a swim on her own and swam ashore somewhere.'

Morag gasped and covered her mouth. 'But instead, she drowned.'

Bruce McNab choked back tears. 'And the useless idiot that I am, I didn't have the gumption to come forward. I just kept quiet.'

'Why did you wait to put flowers on her grave after so long?' Morag asked.

'We had a run in with Dr Dent the other morning. I suppose it unsettled me, brought it all back and I felt guilty.'

'But what I don't understand, Sandy, is why you didn't just have it out with Bruce McNab? Why all this?' She pointed at Bruce McNab's bruised and bloody face and the water-soaked bathroom.

'I wanted him to suffer a bit. I couldn't understand why he hadn't said anything. Especially when he had kept some of her things.' And from a pocket of his track suit he drew out a locket and chain. 'There's a picture of my mum and Heather's dad in here. My mum gave her that one birthday.'

Bruce McNab buried his face in his hands. 'I loved her. I didn't know who broke into my place and stole it, or why. Except that they had come looking for it. I thought you were coming to kill me.'

'I didn't know that would be here,' Sandy said. 'I was just looking for something of hers to confirm that you knew her. And the more time that we spent fishing and all that rot, when you didn't seem bothered about anything, well, it just made me want to make you suffer. To understand what it must have been like for her.'

Morag stood up and looked Sandy straight in the eye. 'Were you going to drown him, Sandy?'

He returned the look, his eyes registering nothing but sorrow. Then he shook his head. 'No. I just had to make a gesture for Heather.' He shrugged his shoulders. 'Family honour, I suppose.'

VI

Torquil slowly turned round and looked at the gun held steadily in Alec Anderson's hands.

'Are you responsible for these bodies?' he asked.

'Only one of them, although I have to admit that I put them both in there.' He smiled. 'Oh and I would appreciate it if you would put your hands up. I haven't decided on the best way of disposing of you yet.'

Torquil raised his hands. 'I think you should put that gun down and we can talk.'

'We can talk well enough like this, Torquil McKinnon.' He backed across the room, all the time keeping the Glock pointed at Torquil's head. He picked up the bottle of Glen Corlan and uncorked it with his teeth, then poured a hefty shot. He took a swig and then returned to face Torquil.

'How long has Guthrie Lovat been dead?' Torquil asked.

Alec shrugged. 'About ten months. The old fool had to go and have a stroke or a heart attack as we were unloading the *Sea Beastie*. Just dropped dead at my feet.'

'And why didn't you just call for help?'

Alec Anderson laughed. 'Are you kidding me? We had been business partners for five years. How would I explain the load of heroin in the boat?'

Torquil's eyes widened. 'Heroin? On West Uist?'

'Aye, heroin on West Uist!' he repeated

sarcastically. 'You may not think it, Inspector, but this idyllic wee island of yours is a sort of *'traffic island'*! How do you think old Guthrie became so rich? From his driftwood sculptures? Away with you. We collect the goods from the buoys that they fling off the cargo boats as they go up and round to Scandinavia. It has been the perfect cover all these years.'

'And so Guthrie Lovat died and I suppose you have been pretending that he's still here.'

'That's right. I've even wired up a tape-recording on the intercom system to discourage visitors. Only Alec Anderson ever visits here to deliver his supplies and to collect his packages of artwork to send all over the world. Only it is heroin not driftwood.' He smirked and took another swig of whisky. 'And I've been chained to this for the last ten months until I worked out the old fool's account number.'

'What account?'

'His numbered Swiss account. The wee place that our suppliers post money into. The old sod would never give me that, he just gave me my cut. But after he died I couldn't get at it at all, until I found the account number. Only by then that Digby Dent bastard was bleeding me dry.'

'He was blackmailing you? About Guthrie?'

'He was. He had seen me drag his body up

the beach from the jetty. I don't think I did it too gently, actually. But he had also seen me that other time, when Guthrie was still alive and I moved a dead body.'

'That will have been Heather McQueen.'

Alec Anderson smiled. 'Right you are. Although we didn't know who she was. She complicated things by drowning and getting washed up like any old piece of flotsam and jetsam on Half Moon Cove. Well, anyway, Dent had been skulking about in the early morning, checking on midge swarms or something, and he saw me do it. Then after the Fatal Accident Inquiry, he started putting the finger on us. Nothing too serious, but enough to hurt. And then a month after Guthrie died he told me that he knew all about it. He even had photographs.' He grinned. 'The fool told me that he had them on his computer.'

'You planned to kill him, then?'

'He pissed me off! Then he implied the other morning that he was going to say something on the TV show — *Flotsam & Jetsam*. He demanded whisky, so I gave him a bottle loaded with a little heroin. I thought he wouldn't make the show. But when he did and he seemed out of control, he had to go.'

'And so you killed him?'

There was a crackling noise from a bench

in the corner, then a tinny voice.

'Alec, it's me!'

Almost immediately there was a whirr and a taped voice spoke out: '*No hawkers, sales folk or onion Johnnies, thank you.*'

'Piss off, Alec and let me in!'

Alec laughed and walked sideways to the bench. He pressed a button. 'Come in, Agnes. We have company.'

'Agnes is in on everything?' Torquil asked.

'Everything. She aspires to living somewhere hot, without having customers to serve. She distracted Digby Dent the other night and I bounced a gnome off his head.'

'And did you both drown him in the tank?'

'We did. And when she gets here we will have to decide how we are going to deal with one very nosy police inspector.' He smiled. 'After all, now that we have access to the account there is nothing to hold us to this god-forsaken wee island any more.'

The sound of the emporium van on the gravel outside was followed by the opening and closing of its door, then a few moments later Agnes Anderson came in. Her face was surprisingly unmoved by the spectacle of her husband aiming a gun at Torquil's chest. There was annoyance rather than surprise.

'Oh Christ!' she moaned. 'Now we have another one.'

'Agnes wasn't happy with me when I told her I had to get rid of that Ferguson clown,' Alec Anderson explained.

He cocked his head to the side. 'What do you think, my love? Is there room enough for three in that freezer?'

'Alec, you're a fool. We can't just shoot him. How can we dump his body with a bullet in it?'

'Is that what you are planning to do with the others? Dump them?'

'Of course,' Alec replied. 'The freezer would keep them well preserved, so we were going to dump them in water somewhere. Somewhere away from here.'

'You had practice there,' Torquil replied. 'A pity that you moved both of them to the wrong places. We have all the evidence we need.'

'Like hell you do!' Agnes said.

Torquil looked past them to the door. Then suddenly he called 'Here, boy!'

There was a noise of running feet then a streak dashed from the door straight for the gap between Alec and Agnes Anderson.

Agnes immediately gasped and shied away and Alec stared down.

It was the slightest chance, but Torquil took it. He kicked at Alec's wrist and the Glock discharged a burst and then went flying from his hand. Torquil instantly flew at Alec and grabbed him in a bear hug.

'Agnes! Get the gun!' cried Alec Anderson. 'Shoot him.'

As Torquil and Alec went over and started grappling on the floor Agnes made a grab for the Glock.

But Crusoe was there before her. Sensing it was dangerous and that he must not let her have it, he sank his teeth into her hand. She screamed and tried to dislodge him, but he clung on.

Torquil brought his head down sharply on Alec Anderson's face and nasal bones snapped in a torrent of blood. Then as the fight went out of the emporium owner he swiftly handcuffed him.

'Leave, Crusoe,' he said. And as the dog dutifully released the terrified Agnes, he handcuffed her to her husband. 'Thank you for letting Crusoe in when you arrived, by the way,' he said to her.

Standing and getting his breath back, he reached for his mobile and called Morag. Briefly he told her of his catch.

'Can you give Ralph McLelland a call? I think we need his ambulance and his assistance. We had better deal with the casualties first, then we had better do the forensics.' He reached over and closed the bench freezer.

He sighed. 'And I am afraid that I don't relish telling Chrissie Ferguson the news that we have found her husband.'

VII

Later that afternoon, the immediate problems and tasks had been tackled, including the arrest of Geordie Innes, who had been implicated by Craig Harrison and Tosh Mulroy as the boss of their antiques robbery gang. The young producer had an expensive drug habit that he had fed by arranging the theft of antiques that had been presented to the *Flotsam & Jetsam* show. A profitable business, they had been working the scam for two seasons.

Then had come the harrowing identification of Fergie Ferguson's body by Chrissie Ferguson, and her subsequent sedation in the cottage hospital by Dr Ralph McLelland.

And it had been an unwelcome solution to the mystery of Crusoe being cast adrift to discover that Rab McNeish the local carpenter and undertaker, had been systematically abusing stray and stolen cats and dogs. Ralph was of the opinion that an animal phobia and a disease phobia sparked by his brother's death from toxoplasmosis had resulted in a psychotic mental illness.

'I knew there was something odd about those knots that I found on the cord he used to lash Crusoe to the timber,' Torquil had confessed to Ralph. 'They were just like those knots that you used after the post-mortem on Dr Dent.'

'Surgical knots,' Ralph had replied. 'A lot of undertakers use them when they tidy up corpses.'

Torquil had just made up his report on all of the cases when Lorna called on her mobile.

'I don't know when Superintendent Lumsden will let me home,' she said. 'That big job that we were working on with the Customs folk came to nothing. He was expecting to make a big drugs bust. Heroin.'

'Tell me more,' Torquil urged.

'He was sure that drug traffickers were using one of the Scandinavian shipping lanes that go past the Hebrides. We boarded one of them with the Royal Navy today, but found nothing. The boss is as angry as I've ever heard him.'

'Perhaps if I tell him about the double murder here on West Uist he might cheer up.'

'A double murder! Oh, Torquil, don't make him any angrier.'

'We solved them both!' And he roughly ran

through the various cases.

'That might help. You know how he is about his crime figures. But I know he was hoping for great things from the drugs case.'

'An MBE, you said. Well, it just happens that we have a heroin haul here. He was right, they have been using one of the shipping lanes, but they have been jettisoning the drugs near West Uist all this time.' He laughed. 'Tell the superintendent that he can have all the glory if he lets you have your leave.'

'I think it would be better coming from you, darling.' And they fell into their usual exchange of intimacies and endearments.

'Maybe I will give the superintendent a ring now,' Torquil said at last. 'Hearing his dulcet tones will end what has been a less than perfect day.'

12

Torquil had never been so glad to make it to Friday night. The scandal and horror went like wildfire around all of the Western Isles, fuelled by Calum Steele in the West Uist Chronicle and his new girlfriend and assistant editor, Cora Melville.

After a meal of roast rabbit and home-made apple pie, washed down with half a bottle each of claret, he and Lachlan sat on opposite sides of the fireplace nursing a large dram of Glen Corlan. Crusoe lay curled up at Torquil's feet.

'I was surprised to learn that old Kenneth Canfield had an alcohol problem,' Lachlan mused.

'Aye, you can never tell by appearances, can you? I have learned that much these last few days. I would never have thought that Alec Anderson and Agnes could be such cold-blooded killers.'

'A shock, right enough,' Lachlan said, sipping his drink. 'And what about Sandy King? Is Bruce McNab going to press charges?'

'No. I think he's accepted it all as a punishment. I don't think he'll ever get over the affair.'

'And how is Morag?'

Torquil grinned. 'In seventh heaven, I think. She and Sandy King seem to have something special going there, although it won't be easy for them with him having to be with his team all week.'

'I am pleased for them. Morag has not had an easy life. But what about that business chappie, the Dundee fellow? Was there anything in the match-fixing stuff? I saw Cora's article about it.'

'Nothing substantial.'

Crusoe suddenly sat up and pricked up his ears.

'What about Rab McNeish? Will there be charges?'

'I don't know,' Torquil replied, reaching down and stroking the dog. 'That's up to the Scottish SPCA, not us. All I can say is it was a grand day that I found Crusoe washed up on St Ninian's Cove. He saved my life.'

'And so now can I take it he'll be staying with us?'

Torquil raised his glass and took a sip. 'That depends on Lorna, I think.'

Crusoe sat up and started wagging his tail. Then he gave a short bark.

'What depends on me?' came Lorna's voice from the hall.

'Lorna!' Torquil cried, jumping up and

running to sweep her into his arms.

'I thought I would surprise you. The boss let me have my time after all, now that he's making his name for that drug clean-up. They're tracing the suppliers all the way back to South America. He might get his MBE one day.'

Crusoe sat down and barked.

'And who is this?' Lorna asked, bending and stroking his ears. 'He's a bonny dog.'

'He saved my life, Lorna.'

'You're joking. Tell me about it.'

'Later,' Torquil replied. 'It's a long shaggy tale.' He kissed her and she kissed him back.

Lachlan gazed ceilingwards and sighed. 'Come on, Crusoe. They might be some time. Let's go and see if we can scare up a rabbit or two on the golf course.'